D1525993

GETTING TO
PHOENIX

GETTING TO PHOENIX

Michael Boloker

Writers Club Press
San Jose New York Lincoln Shanghai

Getting to Phoenix

All Rights Reserved © 2001 by Michael Boloker

No part of this book may be reproduced or transmitted in any form
or by any means, graphic, electronic, or mechanical, including
photocopying, recording, taping, or by any information storage retrieval
system, without the permission in writing from the publisher.

Writers Club Press
an imprint of iUniverse.com, Inc.

For information address:
iUniverse.com, Inc.
5220 S 16th, Ste. 200
Lincoln, NE 68512
www.iuniverse.com

ISBN: 0-595-18781-1

Printed in the United States of America

This book is dedicated to the love of my life, Judy, who was with me every step of the way. Yes, wow!

Contents

1

How it started

It's July of 2000 and I'm established in my Paradise Valley home. I've taken a lot of ribbing from my old New York friends about the name but in a way it is Paradise to me, although the events of the past year have tainted this a bit. It's 106 degrees outside, a blinding, bright sunny day as are most days here and for the first time in a year I don't feel like I'm living in a hotel! This is my home now, at last, and even though I bought this tri-level townhouse as a resale, it seems as if I built it brick by adobe brick—every tile, door handle, paint coat, rug fiber, appliance, sink washer. Even had to buy a new kitchen sink! Every piece of furniture, painting, wall covering my wife and I designed, selected or bought. Every shrub chosen and planted. It started in the summer of 1998, nearly 2 years ago, and time didn't fly when I was having 'fun'! It took a long time to get here and, believe me, it wasn't easy.

Actually it started the first time I ever saw a Gene Autry western movie when I was a boy in Brooklyn going to the Saturday matinee for 25 cents at the Beverly Theater on Church and MacDonald Avenues. Of course we kids got 10 cartoons, a Three Stooge comedy and a Batman serial too. This was preceded by a 65 cent chow mein special at the Nom Tong Chinese Restaurant or a hot dog and knish at Gorelick's deli. Those were good eats for us kids then. But the matinee was the highlight on those weekend afternoons. Seeing Champion galloping across those deserts, climbing those mountains was thrilling. It wasn't like listening to the Lone Ranger on the radio. You could actually see the West. I knew I was going to be a cowboy and live in Arizona when I grew up. There was no doubt about it! Now it's actually happened. Well, not all of it exactly. I'm not a cowboy but I do live in Arizona and I have a 7 foot saguaro cactus by my front door. I do wear cowboy boots even though I haven't been on a horse since I rode at a Pennsylvania boys' camp when I was 13. But I intend to try it again soon, if I can beat the developers to the ranches left in North Scottsdale. I'm a 57 year old retired high school English teacher who left the four seasons of Long Island, New York for the Valley of the Sun!

Being from New York City originally, I learned it is a citizen's requirement to go on vacations to Florida. I think it's written in the New York City charter or something. Perhaps there's a chromosome in the genes that calls Brooklynites to Miami Beach once the snow falls. Thus it was for most winter vacations during my working years. Through the generosity of my wife's rich uncle we managed to finagle 3 trips to an exclusive North Miami resort that I could never afford. The life style was pure luxury and every time I had to return to the cold climate of New York and my teaching job I would suffer through a month of depression. I hungered for the sun and temperatures in the 90's, winds blowing through the palm fronds. My wife called this affliction the 'Turnberries' after the name of the resort at which we stayed. As I hit the 'Big 50' we began to think about retirement. The one advantage career teachers have is being able to retire at the age of 55. The other is having those ten-week summer vacations. Both are good training for retirement. There are teachers who actually know how many days they have to reach this great day, often five or more years in advance. The only thing I can equate it to in my experience is a soldier's count down of short time until his discharge. It's not that teachers dislike their jobs, but like all human beings, who can resist the idea of the lure of those golden retirement years: not having to wake up at 6 A.M., marking papers endlessly, facing down teenagers, doing your five teaching periods a day, forty weeks a year, for 32 years. How many times can one teach "The Adventures of Huckleberry Finn"? I know the work better than Mark Twain!

Therefore beginning in the summer of 1993 we began traveling to perspective retirement areas around the country scouting, like Tonto of that venerable show of my youth. I knew Florida wasn't the place for us—too humid, crowded and old. Seattle was fun but too rainy and dark. California had too many problems similar to those in New York and prices in San Francisco made Sutton Place pale by comparison. Finally we travelled to Phoenix in August of all times! Teachers go when they can and this is when we 'can.' The heat didn't bother me. As long as I'm not in a classroom and can wear shorts, a tee shirt and sandals I'm loose.

We arrived in Phoenix, picked up our bags and rental car and got our first taste of desert browns and fifty shades of tan. When I saw my first Saguaro cactus it was love at first sight. I was back in my Gene Autry western! I could be a cowboy at 55!

Why would I bother to write of my struggles and travails to settle here? I'm not rich and famous. I can't dunk a basketball, pitch no hitters or shoot that puck. I'm not Tom Cruise handsome nor any kind of celebrity. But I am just like those hundreds of Americans who move into the Valley each day to make a new life here. What I went through they all will too, or already have. So here's my tale of "Getting to Phoenix." I trust you will empathize, commiserate and recognize a common experience.

2

Hooked on models

We had trouble finding our hotel along Scottsdale Road because there are few signs and those are understated to blend in with the landscaping. I drove past the Sheraton three times before I asked a fellow at a gas station, a matter of hurt pride to a man, despite my wife's continual pleas to stop and ask directions. What male who can read a map would ever do this? To my chagrin I was actually directly across the street from the hotel. So much for male pride. The hotel was relatively empty and I was conspicuously the only man in the dining room the first night wearing a tie and jacket. I had my first lesson in desert dressing.

Over the course of the first few days we familiarized ourselves with old Scottsdale, were disappointed in downtown Phoenix. We wondered where everybody was during business hours? The streets seemed deserted and the few tall buildings made us realize there's no place like New York. We were amazed at the little towns in the north valley. Carefree and Cave Creek were charming and the Boulders was something out of a tour book. I loved looking up wherever I was and seeing the mountains and the colors, especially at sundown, were astounding. There really were purple mountains majesty. The pinks, reds and oranges of the sky were nothing short of embraceable. They seemed to be whispy clouds of colored powder tinting the heavens in a magical dreamlike display. The valley was growing more appealing by the minute. We were getting the fever and beginning to want this…now!

We had this happen many times before, on many vacations. The first time we traveled to Switzerland we fell in love with a town near Interlachen called Gruendelwald. It was the early seventies and condominiums were a new concept. For $40,000 we could have a two bedroom apartment facing Lake Geneva. Forget the fact that I made $30,000 a year and couldn't speak a word of French, German or Italian. We lived an ocean away, but we actually believed we could swing this: vacation here in the summers, Christmas and Easter and rent it out the rest of the time. Finally we sat down and figured out the costs of travel, taxes, the Berlitz School, time wasted and realized it was a nice dream, but impossible. Maybe some day…

Then it happened again in Florida in 1987. This time it was an $80,000 condo in Palm Beach. We were hot to trot—only 10 years until retirement. I now made $50,000 a year. It was only 2 ½ hours by plane and my in-laws could use it in the winter and pay us for it. This was a presumption on my part. Not only don't we get along well, but who could tolerate them as tenants? And then who wanted to live in Florida in the summer? And ten years is a long time to wait. Something better would come along. So…we passed on this opportunity too!

So with this tainted past, we visited Tucson and didn't find it to our liking although we did go to the Desert Museum and Old Tucson and played the tourist game there. It was fun in a kinky way. I was kind of embarrassed to fall prey to the simulated gun fights and the cowboy and cowgirl actors. We were two of the few not walking around with a camera. But we did play the game and for two hours it was amusing. It was a touristy thing we would never do again. Cowboys shot at each other and fell off second story verandas, wagons and boarded sidewalks plopping into hay wagons, water troughs and dusty streets. God, they must be black and blue! It was a more sophisticated version of cowboys and Indians than we had played as kids. The one event that did capture us was driving off the highway going west on a nondescript Speedwell Road to get to these attractions, wondering if we were lost until we started climbing and then hooked around a mountainside curve and faced a vista that literally took our breaths away. You could see for miles down into a valley covered with saguaros and desert plants. Off in the distance was Old Tucson, the only evidence of man as far as the horizon. This was the west of John Wayne and I imagined coming through here as a pioneer in the nineteenth century and seeing this panorama. Could it have been any less exciting for those people as it was for us?

Upon returning to Phoenix for the second week of vacation we started to get the 'Turnberries.' Everywhere we drove there were signs for new housing developments, planned communities. The newspapers were filled with advertisements. There seemed to be realtors on every corner but we weren't ready for them. First we decided to go house viewing ourselves to get the lay of the land. How much house could you get for the money? What were the best neighborhoods? Was new better than old? We were babes in the desert and we had to do some home-work to get a feel for the place. Of course we knew I had another year of work before we could move here. The spring would be the best time to look, figuring we could find a place, sell our house in New York and have time to move when school was over. That was the logical thing to do. And of course we would rent for a while before we actually commit-ted to the area. Live here, learn the customs, feel out the place…make a few friends, then decide if this was the place for us. Everything done coolly and sanely, well planned and sensible…Right!

On our exploration of Scottsdale the further north we drove the larger the developments. "Planned communities" they were called. Nothing but newly scraped, flat desert, measured out in 60 x 100 foot plots around washes and arroyos, although I hadn't yet learned what these were.

At the sales centers the presentations were professionally Madison Avenue slick and guaranteed to hook potential buyers. I felt like a fish about to bite the worm masking the deadly hook. A newly planted tree lined avenue directed you to a pavilion which you had to pass through to get to the models. Flags flew, music played inside and out, photos, topographical maps and aerial photos were everywhere. The golf course was already in, surrounding the models like a green boa constrictor. You were given a packet of maps, floor plans, price lists, options, community guides as well as a questionnaire which would lead to your getting mail from the builder for the next decade. There were special incentives—a free pool if you bought today (actually a kidney shaped enlarged bathtub), a fireplace (who needed one in 110 degree heat?},10% if you took a mortgage with the builder, free balloons, hats, tee shirts. One even gave free packages of Huggies for young couples with newborns. Maybe they had "Depends" for elderly incontinent retirees? We soon started falsifying the surveys to avoid future calls and mailings and even got downright insulting at pushy sales people. I had ten aliases by 3 P.M. I just wanted to see the models and avoid the spiel, and soon was flat outright honest. "No! I'm just looking. I'm not ready to buy. I'll let you know if I am."

The people in these sales centers are too damned nice. They smile, yes you to death, are polite beyond belief, give you only the most positive responses. I frankly started to doubt if they were human.

And the models were luscious. One even had a 25 x 50 theater with its own popcorn machine and a giant screen suitable to a multiplex theater. From a half million down to the low $100,000's they were so alluring that it was difficult not to like them…and want them…now.

We were amazed by their size. Most were at least 3,000 square feet. 4 bedrooms, 3 car garages, 30 foot ceilings, huge panoramic windows. These were 'Western' houses. As Easterners we were astounded that people needed so much space. And to top it all off, the houses were often built in rows, one on top of the other. And the materials used were so chintzy. They were framed, covered with composition board plywood and chicken wire, stuccoed and topped with Spanish tiled roofs. It seemed as if a good wind would blow them over, but as the salesman said, "There ain't no hurricanes in the desert, nor snowstorms neither!" I guess he was right and I sure wanted to get away from those babies!. On the other hand, who wanted to spend this kind of money for a Levitt house?

Of course we learned, as in all places, that 'location, location' is the key. The farther into the desert we went, the cheaper the price. But who wanted to live in a row house of 5,000 homes, all looking alike, behind walls and gates in the middle of nowhere? There were practical matters too. How do you change light bulbs 50 feet above the floor? How does one dust up in the Alps? It must be a fortune to air condition the Howe Caverns. What do I put in a three car garage besides my Toyota Corolla?

And then we're New Yorkers. I want to be near restaurants, movies, stores, theater, libraries, professional sports teams. These houses were beautiful, but 'you can't eat atmosphere' as the old Horn and Hardhart commercials used to state. This was not for us.

In 1978 my wife and I had bought a dilapidated 125 year old carriage house on the north shore of Long Island which took us two years to make liveable. It was a labor of love and for 20 years after we were happy to have done it up beautifully. Oh, we put up with cracked plaster, creaky floors,dust and drafty hallways. We even had to dig up and replace a 2,000 gallon, buried oil tank. We tolerated antiquated plumbing, noisy baseboard heating, but the house was solid, unique and had character. We were proud of it.

Now, when we retired, we wanted a change. We wanted crisp, new, modern…and smaller. Two bedrooms, one story, a den, some closet space. We wanted to be able to walk to town, be near culture. There would be no babies, kids, dogs. And it must be affordable.

UDC, Ryland, Edmonds, Lewis, Brown, Monterey, Greystone, Del Webb, DC Ranch, Richmond American, Pulte were all wonderful builders…but not for us. We spent a week looking and liking, but we realized if Phoenix-Scottsdale was to be our future home, we had to go in another direction. Perhaps a resale…perhaps an area we hadn't seen yet. We had a year. We would give it a lot of thought and come back Easter time to seriously look, at least for a rental. We would put our New York house on the market and take it from there.

Then with 2 days left on our visit, a little discouraged at not having found what we wanted all week, we accidentally got a lead to the 'promised land.'

Old Scottsdale has rejuvenated itself by becoming a gallery center for Western art. Main Street has rows of shops featuring every variation of Indian and cowboy paintings and sculptures from the very best to the worst 'knock offs.' I personally think most of the stuff looks like enhanced Red Ryder comic book panels, but then what do I know about it. I don't understand the appeal of Picasso either.

So we were cruising through a gallery when my wife and I started a conversation with an attractive, middle aged sales woman. She wore the costume of the sophisticated artiste representative—long skirt, cowboy boots, fringed blouse adorned with silver and turquoise Indian jewelry. Of course as soon as we opened our mouths she knew we were from New York or New Jersey. Maria had moved here 20 years ago from Manhattan. We were familiar with her old Eastside neighborhood and that triggered off a half hour of her oral autobiography which seems to be a requisite for all Arizona store personnel.

We reciprocated and told her about our liking the area and looking to move here in a year but being in a dilemma about finding a 'small place' near town and the city. We wanted something colorful, manageable and reasonable…maintenance free if possible…in other words, a New York apartment in Arizona.

And then she said the magic words. "You ought to come over to see where I live. It's 5 minutes from here. Called the 'Casbah.' Used to be an old movie star's estate. Converted to condo's ten years ago. I've got 2 bedrooms. a fireplace, pools and tennis. Sunday they have open houses. You ought to drive over." And she gave us her address and telephone number.

Tomorrow was Sunday. We had nothing to lose. Our flight back to New York was at 7:30 P.M. We would go to look. We joked about the old Charles Boyer movie for the rest of the night. "Come with me to the Casbah." And we did…

3

A stranger in paradise

True to its name the 'Casbah' did look like our idea of a Moroccan village. The circular gated community was built around a series of winding lanes heavily planted with varieties of cactus, trees that were uniquely blossomed in purples, orchid pinks and whites, gigantic palm trees and tall Oleanders. The gate guard directed us to unit 207 which had the open house and we inched along , gawked out both windows at a row of attached adobe villas, each differently structured, some one storied, others two. The fronts had car ports or spaces and island gardens. 207 was fronted by the largest coleus and philodendron plants I had ever seen. We parked next to 2 tennis courts, wind screened and surrounded by hedges of pink and white Oleanders, red flourishes of Bougainvilleas. There was a 25 meter two-laned lap pool behind a green gated fence. We peeked in and saw a jacuzzi, dressing cabanas, lounge chairs, a barbecue beehive fireplace and a covered patio area. Orange trees grew along the perimeter. The walls looked like turrets on a Spanish castle and when we looked toward the center of the complex we saw a gigantic white onion dome atop a minaret. The building looked like an Islamic mosque. I expected to see Charleton Heston riding toward us as El Cid. We looked at each other, not speaking, but sensing we had found our special place.

We entered through a heavy, rich mahogany arched door and stopped short as the hall opened into a huge great room with a floor to ceiling fireplace, French doors opening at the end of the room onto a patio. The floors were leather colored terra cotta tiles. There were 2 flights of 6 steps, one up and the other down. The realtor, a short bearded man named Russell by his name plate, greeted us. He was perceptive enough to read our faces, eyes open, looking everywhere, mouths open, salivating at the ambiance.

"Quite a place, isn't it?"

"My God," was all I could say.

"Built in the 1930's by a famous Hollywood producer as a weekend retreat. Huge estate. Rumored that Gable and Gary Cooper used to spend vacations here as his guest." He produced several 8 X 10 glossy photos of Jean Harlow look a likes from the old days wearing one piece bathing suits, lounging beneath palm trees by a huge swimming pool. "Place was sold in the 60's to Ramada and then 10 years ago to this builder who converted it into 100 units, all different. Of course its been updated. New plumbing, electrical wiring. Why don't you look around?"

There was an office upstairs which overlooked the great room. Sky lights. Natural wood beamed ceilings and timber posts as supports. Off the great room was a galley kitchen, laundry room, dining room. Down one level was a bedroom suite with its own bathroom and closet. The master bedroom was at the rear of the main level and had a view of the backyard with its own fountain. The massive end of a mountain loomed. We later learned this was Camelback Mountain, a Phoenix landmark. There was a walk in closet and bathroom with 2 vanity sinks, a huge bathtub all tiled in creamy saltillo. Windows were everywhere. The walls looked irregular and when I pointed this out to my wife Russell informed us they were 'soft walls' to make the place look authentically adobe southwestern. There were built in shelves, book cases, a multiplicity of cabinets and crannies in every corner. The place reeked of charm. Berber rugs covered the bedroom floors and the Sante

Fe motif of Indian artifacts and western paintings was embellished by the pink, sand and turquoise upholstery on the heavy furniture. We both knew we could live here.

Russell waited for us. "Place has been on the market for 2 days and I have a couple coming in an hour to put down earnest money and sign the papers. These come up so rarely. They go fast. Historical, you know."

We talked. "How much is it?"

"$335,000. And it's a fair price. You can't buy this kind of ambiance any more. Place is one of a kind. People here from all over the world. Writers, politicians, artists. Even a Phoenix Suns basketball player. You should walk around, see the gardens and the other pools. Here's a map."

$335,000 was about $125,000 more than we could afford or wanted to. But the size was perfect. 1850 square feet. And the lay out was so eclectic. He gave us a fact sheet. Taxes $1600…In New York we paid $7,000. Maintenance fees to the home owners association were $225 a month. My friends in New York City paid $375 for a studio apartment. You could walk to Old Scottsdale, were 2 blocks from the Phoenician Hotel and the place was a knockout.

"Are there any other units available?"

"Not now, but I can show you 2 smaller places that we rent out. When do you plan to move?"

We told him the truth. "Next July and we hoped not to spend that much money."

"Well go look at l07 and 110. Walk around."

We did. We rambled along a series of bricked pathways, twisting from one lovely area to another. The place looked like a set from a Tarzan movie. Trees and shrubs covered rock gardens, walled yards. Orange and grapefruit tree. grew abundantly and olive trees too. We came upon the huge pool from the old photos we had seen and then walked to the mosque. Thus, we later learned, was once the music room to the mansion. It had been converted by a television producer of a popular sitcom into a plush hideaway. The onion dome had been built by the original owner as a marker for his wife to locate when she flew her private plane from California. There had been an air strip on the property then. Something everyone needs.

The more we roamed the more we were astounded by the beauty of the 'Casbah' and the richness of the grounds.

The coup de grace hit us as we passed through an archway into the central quad surrounded on 3 sides by 2 stories of what looked like a Mexican hacienda. There was a lush lawn split into quadrants. Roses bloomed along the crossed pathway in an 'x' of color. The bouquet from the petals permeated the air and in the center of this was a water fountain tiled in white and blue of an Indian maiden kneeling to pour water from a ewer.

We peeked into the two small apartments off the rose garden. One was a smaller version of the unit we had seen, with a living room, kitchen and garden downstairs. A huge tiled staircase spiraled up to a bedroom loft with patio. The other was a one bedroom suite. Each was about 1500 square feet but gave a more spacious illusion. Wood, adobe and tile were prominent. They were too small for our needs even though the prices were within our range.

When we got back to Russell we asked why people didn't buy these. "They're good investments for speculators. And it takes a special person to want to live here. It's older, smaller. There are few, if any children. No garages. People today want big. New!"

"We know. We've been looking. 207 would be ideal, but its a bit high for us and it's really too early. The spring would be ideal."

He was friendly enough and we talked about our jobs and home back east. He was a good listener. "You should look around the Biltmore area. There are some lovely places there too. The hotel and the Wrigley Mansion. But anyway, give me your name and number and I'll keep an eye out for you."

"Sure," I thought. "Like we'll ever hear from this guy again. We're New Yorkers, friend, not hicks from Kansas."

So we left. Even drove around the Biltmore area as he suggested, but our hearts weren't in it. We now had the 'Casbahs.' The place was a treasure, a paradise, and we wanted in. But was it possible? We returned to the hotel and packed.

It was a long plane ride home.

4

Kids and dogs, God bless 'em!

Our last fling of the summer was a Labor Day trip to San Francisco to visit my son, a pediatric resident, another word for slave. He works 90 hour weeks for $35,000 a year at a hospital in the East Bay area near Berkeley. We had two free frequent flyer tickets and used them to cross the continent on one of those wonderful six hour plane rides that takes nine and serves pretzels, soft drinks and cramped seats. Two stops, guaranteed one lost suitcase, perhaps a missed connection. It's funny how we had begun using our credit card to buy everything from toothpaste to paying medical bills all with the idea of earning miles. The airline gives you two seats on any flight Wednesday or Thursday from midnight to 3 A.M. with stops in three airports along the way. There are four tickets available on these flights which must be booked six months in advance. Ah the wonders of giveaways! It was easier than writing checks or paying cash, but my credit card bill was so long it could have been serialized. We were happy to be going but dreading the return to work on the Tuesday following the holiday. Phoenix was in the past now, not to be considered until after the winter.

We had been visiting the Bay area for the past seven years because of my son's moving there and searched for places to visit while he worked. One of our favorite haunts was Berkeley which was in a time warp with the sixties. The place reminded me of Greenwich Village in the Beatnik days with bearded and barefoot kids dressed up in ragged jeans, sweaters, and peasant blouses, the women that is, although today one never knows. Street peddlers sold cheap beaded jewelry, incense, dope and played guitars on street corners and the most incredible sight of all was sitting in the quad on the University of California campus and seeing fifty year old hippies still wearing the same clothes they did thirty years ago, literally, making speeches about politics, the environment and equal rights for gays and lesbians as if nothing had changed since the Chicago Seven. I hadn't seen Afros in twenty years! I expected that old character who appeared on Jack Paar's old 'Tonight' show, Gypsy Boots. One exhibitionist dresses only in a loin cloth and lays on a wooden cross for hours without moving. Students nonchalantly walk by. I suppose he's trying to emulate Jesus, but this is taking it too far.

We were whiling away the afternoon when my wife decided to check the messages on our telephone tape at home in New York. I sat munching a piece of pizza in a Telegraph Avenue eatery along with an army of college students, pulling mozzarella cheese strings to outrageous lengths, feeling like a grandfather when I got a major surprise. Russell the realtor from Scottsdale had left a message to call him immediately. Something had come up at the Casbah which was too good to pass up.

We returned his call and he informed us that a unit similar to 207 had just been put on the market, for considerably less money and was worth looking at. We asked him two basic questions. "Why so cheap? What's wrong with it?"

"The owner wants to get rid of it. I went over to look at it this morning. It's basically the same as the one you saw. Just needs some cosmetic work. He has renters who are giving him and the condo association a hard time. He wants to get rid of the place. Not as nice a view from the patio, but I think it's worth your coming down here to look. Needs a little work, that's all. Is there any way you can get out here?"

I didn't really need this now. We were visiting my son who we only saw two or three times a year. We really weren't ready to commit to anything with a year until my retirement. We hadn't yet begun to plan to sell our house in New York. Work was only three days away. It was a depressing thought.

So of course we went the next morning. Southwest Airlines could get us to Phoenix in an hour and fifteen minutes for $39 and we could get back to SanFrancisco that evening. Our son was working during the day anyway so instead of mountain climbing the streets of San Francisco, we would have an adventure..

Russell met us at the airport and wooed us with his smooth Virginia accent and the promise of lunch at Houston's, a restaurant we had come to like for its salads. He was most reassuring. It was twenty minutes from the Airport and when we drove in through the gates of the Casbah I was still skeptical. We drove through the winding lanes to the back of the complex and saw a young girl, perhaps ten, roller blading in front of unit 222. She wore a bikini top which she didn't need yet and bright red shorts, sort of a baby hooker. Ah kids! "You the guys who want to buy this place? Don't. It stinks here!"

A lovely greeting. We approached the door and Russell rang the bell which prompted a dog's barking menacingly. There was no answer so he knocked. Still no response. More barking. The little hooker pushed by and opened the door. "Come on in, if you have to. I'll get Ashley." She preceded us on her skates into the long hallway and disappeared. We waited in the alcove.

The place was dark and a washing machine was churning to the right. An ironing board was set up in the breakfast room and dishes left on a small table. A chain hung from the ceiling with no light fixture attached and the wires exposed. The girl came whizzing back bouncing off the hallways walls, her skates scratching at the tiled floor. "She says you should look around."

What a delightful greeting. We passed through the fifteen foot hall-way into the great room which was similar to the one we had seen before but had an opposite lay out. There were Arcadia sliding doors opening to a small atrium and a narrow yard winding to the back of the unit. The up and down stairs were to the left with a dining room off the living room. There were a pair of huge dark green and red sofas which cluttered up the room and chile strings hanging from each side of the fireplace. This must have been decorated by Gabby Hayes, bunkhouse decor. The screen to the hearth was hanging off. Outside a black chow dog, its purple tongue hanging out of its jowls was jumping against the glass doors tearing the screen and snarling ferociously. "Shut up, Spike. Shut your stupid mouth." The girl smacked the window to make the dog stop but only antagonized it more. "She won't hurt you. She just doesn't like strangers."

We were not reassured but realized we weren't going to see the back yard. I hoped the doors were locked. We went downstairs and stepped into the guest unit which was littered with all manner of trash.. There was a Berber rug there somewhere but it was covered with cellophane bags, potato chips and pretzels which we felt grinding into the carpet as we attempted to step into the suite. Pizza boxes and moldy crusts were scattered about. The bed was unmade, the shade drawn down so that the place was cast in near darkness. It was like a prison cell. We switched on the light but it didn't work. The bathroom door was closed and we pushed it open to find the floor piled with damp towels. At least someone showered here.

We retreated upstairs and preceded to the loft which overlooked the living room. Oops. There was a shirtless, thirteen year old boy lying on a bed with a plastic pistol in his hand. He looked at me and aimed, clicking the trigger. Good thing I flinched. A pellet whizzed over my right shoulder and struck the wall inside some bookshelves, splattering a blot of yellow green paint. "Why you little…" My wife restrained me.

"Sorry. Didn't realize it was loaded." He smirked. You guy's going to buy this place? Take my advice and don't. People stink. Don't let you do anything. Complain all the time. My dad's a lawyer. He's going to sue them."

Russell looked at me and shook his head. I wanted the kid to talk. "You don't like it here?"

"No. Can't play. No bikes, no skating. No kids. There's nothing to do. I can't wait to move." Neither could I.

I decided to be friendly. "Seems nice to me. The house I mean."

"We're having ours built. Supposed to move in soon as its ready. This place ain't bad, but you should see my room in our new place. Twice the size and our own pool. And we'll have horses." I felt sorry for the poor animals.

As Russell lead my wife down the stairs, I remained to talk to the boy. He seemed to have half a brain despite his bad aim and winning personality. I heard the girl skating downstairs across the living room and the dog thudding against the glass doors. Would we get out alive?

"How's the house? Any problems? Bugs? Leaks? You know?"

"It's O.K. I guess. Outside there's bugs. Big. Like this." He spread his thumb and forefinger. "Especially in the summer. You don't want to go out in the summer."

"Anything else? "

"Ask Ashley. She's marrying my dad. Ask her. She's in the back. In the bedroom. My father's at work. Does he know you're here?"

"I'm sure he does, thanks." The boy was playing with the paint pistol again. I figured I'd better leave.

As I descended the staircase I expected one in the back and when it didn't happen I felt lucky. The shades on the boy's window were torn. The dog was still waiting for us to come out, salivating at the prospect of eastern meat. No thanks.

Russell and my wife had disappeared into the back master bedroom as I nosed around the kitchen. The wall paper was pealing off the walls. The ceiling had three light canisters hanging down, relics from the eighties. Kitchen cabinet doors were half open, revealing a mess of cans and boxes. The ceilings were darker wood than those in the unit we had first seen casting a pall over the place. It seemed to be lit like one of those arty films, amber and blurred dark images. The place was depressing me. Compared to the other unit it was like heaven and hell, this being the latter. The layout was intriguing but the litter, the torn shades and screens, the dark ceilings made me claustrophobic. I heard my name called and went back to the master bedroom suite passing the bathroom and walk-in closet. I was afraid to walk in however. The first thing I saw was a Nordic track machine in the corner. The windows had blinds which were closed and there was a large screen television playing a soap opera in the other corner. A king sized bed dominated the room. The ceiling was the same dark wood color, making the room look smaller than it actually was. But the most amazing thing of all was that the bed was occupied by a young woman covered with a sheet up to her waist, wearing an Arizona State tee shirt. "Hi, I'm Ashley. Sorry for the mess but it's early and I haven't gotten around to waking yet. The kids show you around?" She lit a cigarette, blew out match and dropped it on the floor. I guess she saved on ashtrays.

I was aghast. How could she stay in bed with three strangers looking over her house? I guess it's a new world. "Shut up out there!" She turned to us.

"They're not my kids. My fiance's. We're getting married in two weeks. They're an handful, those two. Shut up, Spike, god damn it!" She shouted at the dog. "Surprised my husband let you come in. Can't stand the damned owner. Hassling us. And the association. People never leave us alone. Can't be out soon enough. Could've waited to let realtors in." She threatened us.

I wanted out of here. "Thank you, Miss…We've seen enough." I tugged my wife out, Russell following. I shook my head. No way. This is a wreck. No matter what the price. We stepped outside, glad to be in the sunlight and fresh air. I conferred with my wife. "No. This is a disaster. Too dark. Wrecked. We don't need this."

"Let's walk around back," Russell suggested. We walked past three units and turned the corner of a beautifully landscaped garden filled with aloes, prickly pear cactus plants and saguaros. We turned left down a pathway and peered into three yards, one flag stoned, a second filled with statuary and primitive Mexican wood furniture and the third looking like a vacant lot in New York City. The dog heard us and rushed at the four foot wall. He was too heavy to jump it, thank goodness. There were leaves covering a bricked patio and overgrown shrubs blocking a walkway back along the wall of the house to the atrium. There was litter, dog crap, torn paper everywhere and two garbage cans in the corner near a hose spigot. No wonder the boy said there were bugs out here. With this mutt there might have been body parts here too. How could these people have let this go? I would be embarrassed to live here. The garden, if you could call it that, was an eyesore, but I wasn't surprised after seeing the inside. Little lizards darted across the expanse of trash. Yuch!

"Russell, I don't think so. There's just too much to do. It's dark, in disrepair and the place is a nightmare. I think we've seen enough." My wife looked at me in agreement, but not completely. I could tell she wasn't convinced.

"Look, I realize this looks bad, but I went through it yesterday when the dog wasn't here. I spoke to the owner. They're fining him $25 a day for the tenant's having a dog. That's illegal. And the kids damaged the swimming pool. Shot off the fire extinguishers. He owes nearly $2,000. Their lease is up at the end of September. Owner wants to sell. He bought it for speculation and rented it out only this year. It's been pretty much empty for the other time. He's had it since 1988. So other than this year, the place is pretty new. Just put it on the market for $235,000. It's a steal. If it weren't for his conflict with the landlord, other realtors would be all over it. The two who did come over were afraid of the dog. One nearly got bitten. The words around. So give it a little more thought." Russell said a lot for him, in that syrupy voice. He wasn't pushing hard, just making it seem that the facts were incontrovertible.

"Give us ten minutes, Russell. Let us talk. O.K.?"

"Sure." He went to sit in his air conditioned car. I realized it was damned hot, maybe 100 degrees, and it was September.

We walked back through the cactus garden, watching red birds nesting in a beautiful orchid tree. We passed one beautiful yard after another. The grounds were gorgeous. We got to the center quad again and walked along the roses, sat at the base of the fountain and looked around. "It is within our means. We can sell our house and use the money to buy this one. I can fix it up. I know I can."

"Are you seeing something I'm not? The place is a wreck. It's dark. There's no view from the backyard. We have a year to go. I can't carry two houses!"

"It just needs cosmetic work. Paint, new rugs, furniture. Look around. This place. I want to live here. Let's see if that woman is in. The woman from the gallery." I reluctantly agreed. We found Maria and she invited us into her house which was around the corner from 222. It was done up in Mexican decor with beautiful, colorful paintings covering the walls, bleached white terracotta floors, plants everywhere and a fountain in her backyard. We told her what had happened.

"You're wife is right. Those people have been here for six months and they've been nothing but trouble. The owner is beside himself to get them out. It's costing him money everyday. You can fix the place up easily. You should think about it." We spent ten more minutes making small talk.

We walked back to Russell. "If we buy it, when would we have to close?"

"End of October. Takes about four weeks. Work through the title company."

"Russell, I have to work until next June. I can't afford to carry this and my house in New York."

"We'll fix it up fast. I can rent it out for you until the spring. That should cover your costs. And then you can move in when you're ready."

He made it sound easy. I wanted an excuse to bail out. It was scary actually doing this. "How am I going to clean it up? Fix it?"

"I can take care of it for you. I have people who do this. We'll have the home inspected. Termites, roof, cleaning service. Paint it."

"What about lawyers? The closing costs?" I envisioned my bank account shrinking.

"Not here. In Arizona we close through the title company. No lawyers. You can do it by phone. It'll cost you maybe $700."

"You're kidding. In New York it costs thousands. It's a big hassle. Lawyers, closers. It's like a U.N. conference."

He smiled. "Not in Arizona. I've been here 12 years now. I know what you mean. It's not like that here. Much less complicated."

"But who's going to look after the property?"

"Me. That's my job. I'm not just here today, gone tomorrow. I'll take care of everything. It's where I earn my commission." Russell laughed at us.

This was too good to believe. He drove us to Houstons for a quick lunch. Russell told us about his wife and daughter. His family was still in the Richmond, Virginia area. He loved golf but rarely had time to play. The real estate market was booming. There was little room for anything else for him. It was a pleasant lunch but I felt pressured by the prospect of negotiating, closing, fixing, renting, moving. And we still had to return to San Francisco. It wasn't the way we pictured our last vacation weekend. We had been here for two hours. It seemed a lifetime. We would call Russell that night, at his home, to let him know of our decision.

"Don't wait too long now. It's not going to stay on the market for long. Pray the dog is still there to scare people off."

"Good old Spike. Can you bargain on price? In New York you never pay the asking price."

"They don't do that much here. But make a fair offer and see what happens. The owner is in New York too so he may expect some give and take. Think about it and let me know later." Russell again didn't push. I liked his manner and straight forwardness. Could we believe him? Trust him?

He drove us back to Sky Harbor Airport. We flew back to San Francisco getting more excited by the mile.

5

Steals and deals

We talked it over on the plane ride, so busy with what was happening, figuring costs, planning for the sale of our New York home, coming here for Christmas and Easter vacations, that I forgot to be tense while flying, a first in my life. I must be excited not to imagine the plane's crashing with every bit of turbulence.

That night at dinner we discussed the Arizona possibilities with our son who was thrilled with the idea of our being closer to him if we did move there. He could come on weekends, if he ever got any off. It wasn't a subway ride but really not expensive. Over the hors d'oeuvres we were doubtful. By the main course we were 50-50. At dessert we made up our minds to go for it.

We called Russell at 10 P.M. and told him to offer $200,000. God, if we could get it for that it would make us happy campers. He told us he'd make the offer and call us in the morning.

At 10 A.M. we called from our son's apartment. Russell told us the owner was away for the day at the beach in the Hamptons. Did we know where that was?

Did we know? My God, we lived a half-hour away. If we were in New York we could talk to him face to face. How ironic! Here we were, New Yorkers in California, trying to get a hold of another New Yorker about buying a place in Arizona, using a Virginian to negotiate. We were becoming real jet setters.

Russell told us he had left a message. We gave him our number and told him we'd call later. We waited until noon and finally went back to Berkeley to watch the freak show. At one we called again. "I got the owner and gave him your offer. He came back at $230,000."

"Tell him $205,000." Thrust and parry. This was going to be like buying a car. "How'd he sound?"

"Hard to tell. I'll get back to you."

At 3, after devouring pizza and frozen yogurt we found a telephone booth in the student union and called Russell again.

"$225, and only if we close by the end of the month."

"Wow…$210. Tell him how bad the place is. It needs major work. Yard, paint, carpet, fixtures." Boy, would I like to meet the owner directly.

Look him in the eye. I had been a good poker player. This way it was torture.

We went back to my son's apartment. By five there was still no message. We went to dinner that Saturday night and later took in a movie. When we got back at midnight there was a message from Russell to call him. Did this guy ever go home?

We got his pager and left a message. An hour later he returned our call.. "He came down to 220."

"What do you think?" I was ready to concede. Compared to 335 it was a good deal, I guess.

My wife wasn't about to give in. "Let's play hard ball. We stick with 210."

We slept on that, or tried to. Not only were our heads spinning but I challenge anyone to sleep soundly on a Jennifer convertible!

Sunday morning, 9 A.M. The phone rings. "$215."

"Split it. $212,500."

"He's away until Monday."

"We leave Monday morning for New York. Let us know early or in New York Monday night."

Sunday was a whirlwind trip to Alcatraz, which froze us. After all the years visiting San Francisco we had finally broken down to do the tourist thing. This was a sure sign we were not ourselves. It was the coldest I'd been since the February blizzard. We had no thought of the end of summer, work on Tuesday, saying goodbye to our son for at least four months.

No calls from Arizona the next morning. I anticipated the worst. Was it worth losing a deal for five thousand dollars? It's funny how that much money seems insignificant now, but it's still a lot of money. Who did I think I was, a sports agent? I was half hoping we'd lose the deal, half hoping we'd get it. Either way it would cause me grief and worry, two of my least favorite pastimes.

We landed in New York City on Monday night, the tension having flown with us across the continent, taking our minds off the prospect of work tomorrow.

This was to be my last year of teaching, an exciting prospect, but not as exciting as the house negotiation.

At 10 P.M., 7 P.M. Arizona time, Russell checked in. "$213. Take it. He'll even paint and clean up the place."

"Doesn't he have to?"

"Don't push it. I'm telling you, it's a steal. It'll cost you minimal money to fix it up. Take the deal."

"O.K. Let's do it."

We were in…barring unforeseen complications. In our last house purchase twenty years ago, we learned you don't own a place until the checks clear and the deed's in your hand. We had haggled over a broken window pane at the closing for three hours. It ended up costing the owner an extra $20 on a $52,000 sale. It's hard to believe but it happened. I worried that Arizona might be the same. I hoped I was wrong.

6

Long distance landlord

I often consider myself a dinosaur, a soon to be extinct breed, being 56 years old, a teacher of literature who likes reading a novel over seeing the movie, retains a rotary telephone, writes letters rather than 'E' mail, and goes to a ballgame in person not viewing it on television. Because of this deal I was forced into a world of faxes and Fed Ex, The purchase agreement had to be signed by both the seller and us and therefore we kept running down to Walgreens to use their fax machine at a dollar a page in order to meet deadlines and expedite transactions. The drugstore became my second home for a week but we finally got the agreement signed. We sent earnest money via bank transfer wire, another $15. Russell called us every night to keep us apprised of the situation. He was extremely personable and assuaged our anxiety. He never failed to respond to our calls and always had a sensible answer. He was giving the name of realtor a much needed boost from the stereotype we feared. He was totally accessible. The closing was scheduled for September 30, pending all the usual contingencies. Time sure flies when you're having fun.

There had to be termite and roof inspections, screens repaired where our old friend Spike had a dog fit. The house was to be broom clean inside and out, especially paint splotches dotting the wall in multicolored murals thanks to my young pistol happy friend. There was to be a walk through right before the closing and many documents to get to us concerning radon, the home owners association C C and R's (which we later learned were covenants, conditions and restrictions) and other legalities to be faxed, fed exed and exchanged. Money transfers had to be arranged, deeds prepared, title searches done…and all without lawyers. I was happy about this but still New York skeptical, anticipating the worst.

The C.C. and R's were a night's reading. This is a thick book with every conceivable rule and regulation regarding the complex. The units could only be painted Navajo white with olive trim on the windows. Only Dunn Edwards paint was acceptable No exterior feature could ever be altered without permission of the board of managers. There were rules governing the maintenance of the gardens, the shrubs in one's yard, car parking, swimming pools, tennis courts, pets, bicycles, motor bikes, stereos…Everything but visiting hours and sexual preferences. It was a regular U.S. Constitution, only tougher…but it seemed to be comprehensively strict which we liked in our middle aged conservatism. It looked good. Things appeared to be going so well that we started advertising our home in the New York Times and Long Island Newsday. Of course this meant fielding calls from every realtor within fifty miles. My wife had been a real estate salesperson some years back and she was familiar with the breed. That's why Russell was such a delight. We could have used him here in the East and hoped to avoid going through the trouble of listing our home, instead wishing to sell it ourselves thereby saving a commission from a bloodsucking third party. Our house was going to be difficult to sell because of its age and unusual character. It would take a special person to buy it. I don't want to sound conceited but it would. It had to be someone in the arts or education who liked old classical features, unique architecture and a house with personality. Advertising cost us nearly fifty dollars a week… it was all part of the game of adding up those petty costs.…advertisements, faxes, fed exes, phone calls…but it was all part of our 'steal' and minimal compared to the money we had saved by not buying at the price of unit 207. I told this to myself on a daily basis!

The last week of September things became hectic, or rather more so. Hectic was the norm in my life now. The tenants still had not moved out, prohibiting the inspections. Russell found out that the tenant's house was not ready yet. There was still the matter of the owner's paying the fines for the illegal dog, good old Spike. The homeowners' association would not let any transaction go forward until all matters were resolved. Things were at a standstill.

We wanted the deal but the contract was going to be void if the deal was not closed by September 30. We didn't want to seem anxious, but we didn't want to lose this now. Our hearts and minds were geared to this whole scenario now. We were going forward, selling our house, going to Phoenix on our vacations to set things up for a renovation…renting out the place for the winter as soon as we took title.

Russell handled things well. On October 1st we extended the contract for fifteen days and in turn got the owner to allow us to inspect the roof. It was done and we were told there were three years left on it if it were sealed immediately. Russell got the owner to pay for this and it was to be done within the week. One for us.

The termite inspection was also completed and revealed that there was evidence of termites along the front perimeter of the house and around the carport. Treatment would cost $700. The owner was obliged to pay for this. He didn't like it but it was the law. We were assured that termites were common in this area and there was not structural damage. I thought termites just like Long Island. I guess they too had migrated to warmer climes. Two for us.

By October 7th the tenants were still living in the unit and the seller's attorney was trying to get him out, legally that is. I'm sure Spike was still on duty.

On October 14th they were still there with an accommodation to us forthcoming for another week's delay. This time Russell got the owner to agree to an appliance warranty contract at a cost of $350 for the year. It covered the air conditioner, washer, dryer, dish washer. Only the refrigerator was not included. Three for us.

The closing was now imminent but then we got a disturbing call the night of October 19th. Ashley, the wife had accidentally driven her car into the front wall of the unit and smashed it in damaging the front hall bathroom. It's tough avoiding walls! Interior and exterior work was required entailing sheet rock, removal of the commode, respackling and tiling, and wall papering. This might take another week.

We were obviously not happy about this. Not only were we skeptical about such major damage, but we would be into November and that rental prospect was not going to be easy if we needed more time to spruce up the place and get it ready for showing.

Russell assured us it would be taken care of. We continued worrying. After all someone had to do it. We were locked into a game of hurry up and wait!

Meanwhile, we had a good prospect come in to see our New York home. She was a photographer with a college teaching husband. He taught literature too. We could tell, after many false alarm customers, that she really liked the house. She brought her husband back on the weekend. We were excited about this and even told them of our plans for Arizona. When they asked us what would we do if we had to move out early, we said we would. Of course we hadn't considered this possibility. If we had to get out in 3 months, the usual time for a closing, that would put us into March. Maybe we could work something out, like borrow Spike or drive our car through the garage wall...or have to live for a few months with our in-laws, God forbid! But we were putting our chickens before the egg.

Russell's nightly calls became my wife's therapy but the tenants were still in, the homeowner's association still not allowing any deals to be consummated until all fines were paid, and my anxiety was increasing as the temperatures dipped with the coming of Halloween.

And then, just like that, it happened. The tenants left on October 31. The seller settled all fines. Russell did our walk through inspection. It wasn't great. The wall had been repaired but not repainted and papered. A new hose spigot had to be put in on the front wall. The bathroom tiles needed to be replaced. There was a water leak under the bathroom commode. The rugs were burnt in the back bedroom. Ah, Ashley! The place needed painting and major cleaning. My wife and I had a major argument in which I was very close to canceling the whole thing and then we looked at some photographs Russell had taken and sent to us and got over our second thoughts. "Take care of it all, Russell, and send me the bills. Just get it done so we can rent the place." Were we crazy? Sight unseen—water leaks, dirt, unpainted walls? Who in his right mind would buy into this? We would. It was now an obsession. We were going with our guts, intuition and hope! We did close on November 5th with one thousand dollars held for these repairs and the clean up. It took more wire transferrals to get the money to the title company and we did get the papers signed via our favorite fax machine in Walgreens. The clerk there called me by my first name now and even threw in a free candy bar for our being such frequent customers. I think it would have been cheaper for me to buy my own fax machine. We now learned about Arizona time. Things there do not get done today....they get done...when they get done...manana...or next semana...or more. So it took over a month for the yard to get cleaned up, the rugs shampooed, and Russell to hire a handyman to go in and paint. The man turned out to be very thrifty with our money and we appreciated it.

Now we awaited a renter who would unburden us of the carrying charges for the months until we would move in...hopefully, July 1, 1998. We decided to go down on Christmas vacation to see what the place looked like and then in April to arrange for the work we would want done to make the place ours...new floors, rugs, paint and paper...fix up the garden. My wife was buying decorating magazines by the gross and was brimming with ideas for how we would remodel. We also decided to sell or give away all our furniture, just keeping the mattress and a few odds and ends to get started. We wanted to start fresh and new in the Casbah

This was the plan. It didn't quite work out that way. The couple who we felt so sure about did not call back on purchasing our house. Russell was trying to rent for $1500 a month unfurnished. It was getting no takers, which he couldn't understand. With the Super Bowl being in Sun Devil Stadium this year he would be able to rent it, we were assured. People were renting out garages. But where were our tenants to sleep? Hopefully too drunk to notice the lack of beds. Most renters wanted the place for a year. We didn't want to rent it that long. We wanted to be in in the summer.

When we traveled down to Phoenix on Christmas vacation we saw why the place didn't sell. The rugs, although clean, were stained. The paint job the handyman had done was a splotchy affair of covering up the old paint splotches. It looked like he had done the job with flat paint in some spots and enamel in others. The bathroom was repaired but the yard still looked like an overgrown jungle. Although the place was clean, it was not move in ready. We were disappointed but now resigned ourselves to carrying two houses. We could manage, although it involved a negative cash flow as my accountant told us. But we had no choice now. On Russell's advice, in a last desperate attempt, we lowered the rental fee…Ironically, in March Russell got an offer to rent the place until December and at the original price. We told him no. The prospect even offered to pay $1750. It was tempting, but we were adamant. Our hearts were set to move this summer, to start our new lives.

So we resolved to come back in April for Easter vacation, and carry out arrangements as we had planned. We spent the rest of Christmas in San Francisco…and fortune smiled on us again. The city must be our lucky charm. When we got back to New York there was a call from the couple who had seen the house. They wanted to see it again.

As it turned out they bought it…we went through the whole haggling thing again, agreed on a price, and managed to break even. It would be a wash, no gains or losses…financially that is. The move would occur the first week of April. We managed to rent a one bedroom apartment close to our home from a friend for three months. We would have garage sales in March, hire movers…do the closing…all over again, but things were looking good. We were eager. Russell would check our place every week until the summer.

7

Garage sale

The last Saturday of March we had our garage and tag sale. It was advertised to start at 9 A.M.

The day turned into one of those days of enlightenment. People starting coming at 7 to get the good buys. Two couples were helping us for the cost of a free dinner. By 5 P.M. I had a new slant on the nature of the human animal, 'varietus tag sale shark!'

People wanted bargains, no matter how minor. If an item was $1 they wanted it for 50 cents. They bought clothes I was embarrassed to wear. There is a whole society of warmongers out there who only want knives, guns and Nazi memorabilia. The bund is alive and well on Long Island.

One lady drove up in a Mercedes Benz and proceeded to walk me around for half an hour filling up a wheelbarrow, which she intended to purchase also, with at least 25 items. I kept reminding her of the sticker prices. She nodded as we went along. This was going to be the mother of all sales!. Finally as I totalled the stuff to $125 she informed me that she didn't walk around with that kind of money. Would I take $15 for the lot? Ugatz! I less than politely led her off my property!

A lovely, elderly Hispanic woman bought an old typewriter for her daughter. She wanted the girl to use it for her schoolwork. Obviously didn't have the money for a computer. I had it marked for $25. She was so sweet and excited to be buying this educational wonder that I gave it to her for $5 and threw in a ream of paper.

A young newly married couple, barely speaking English fell in love with our Whiticombe dining room set. Solid oak, 6 chairs and two extension leaves. It originally costs us over $3,000. They had $150 to spend. We told them to come back at 5. If it was still there we would talk. At the end of the sale I had forgotten about them but sure enough, the husband did show up. He told us in broken English they were working in the kitchen of a local restaurant and were in the U.S. from Portugal for only two months. We gave him the furniture for $100, a set of dishes we had ear marked for the garbage. He and a friend loaded the items into their battered truck and left. Three hours later, while we were preparing for bed there was a knock at the front door. I peered out the window and saw the couple downstairs. "Probably going to hold us up." I went down and confronted the young lady. She asked to speak to my wife who approached her nervously.

The girl sincerely hugged my wife and said, "Gracias." My wife gave them another carton of clothes. We felt good about helping these people. The biggest financial success was the sale of my son's collection of baseball, football and hockey bubble gum cards. When he was a boy he and his friends collected, flipped and lived for these Topps cards. They had been in a box in the garage for over 10 years, untouched and barely remembered until I found them a week earlier while cleaning out the place. There must have been 500 of them. I told my son I was going to dump them when we moved unless he wanted me to send them out to California, which would be a pain in the ass. One of my buddies at school told me they were worth money if in good condition. He brought me a catalogue which listed the value of each by year, number and date. They were supposed to be in 'mint condition' to hold their value. I found a Wayne Gretzky rookie card in fair shape. It was allegedly worth $250. Others had an estimated price of $10 to $50, some not. I wasn't about to barter these at a card show so I put out the whole box. Surprisingly a man came up to me in the late morning and offered $200 for the entire collection. Cash! I took it and later sent the money to my son. If the guy made a fortune on the cards, good for him. I was happy with the $200. It's amazing the value some of us place on crap!

When we had moved into our house in 1976 we had been given an artificial willow tree by our best friends. We hated the thing but kept it in in the farthest living room corner in order to sustain the friendship. At last we could get rid of the thing…except nobody bought it. Not for $25…$20…$15. By 4:30 we agreed that whoever sold it for any price would get a drink at dinner. My friend Don sold my son's bedroom set at the last minute. He threw in the tree as a bonus…for nothing. The people had no choice but to take it. It reminded me of the old Texaco Star Theater with Milton Berle when he had Steve Stone fast talking customers…"I'll tell you what I'm gonna do…with your courtesy and kind permission I have here…"We were all of an age to remember those days of early T.V. We laughed over this for a long time. There would be no artificial willow tree in the Casbah!

We ended up making money enough to cover our moving costs, having fun bargaining, giving some nice people 'gifts,' and busting chops on the nasty people who tried to cheat us. The items we didn't sell we gave to charity. Some junk we put out on the curb with the garbage that night. It was gone in the morning. There still are garbage pickers even in suburbia. It hurt most to give up books and trinkets that had been part of our lives for so long. They belonged to us and had sentimental value. They were part of the old house, a term we now used. It was sad in a way—a time bringing on nostalgic memories—but we were looking forward, excited, the unbilical cord to our old carriage house was being cut.

Three months in a one bedroom apartment was inconvenient, but the thought of getting to Phoenix made it tolerable. We had the rest of our lives to look forward to…the dream was becoming a reality!

8

It's Contacts!

On Easter vacation we were so anxious to get to our place that we didn't even stop at the hotel. Getting to Phoenix that Saturday seemed like the longest flight, since we were bursting with anticipation. We actually owned a place down in the desert. It was ours. Our place! It was exciting. We knew no one down there except Russell, the realtor, an insurance agent we had spoken to over the telephone to get house coverage, and a bunch of names on communications with the board of managers of the home owners association.

We found out like Biff Loman in Arthur Miller's "Death of a Salesman" that 'it's contacts, Biff, contacts' if you want to get anywhere in this world. And we turned out to be lucky, after a week of frantic running around to take care of the myriad projects we had to address. We became acquainted with a series of characters who would a lasting effect on our new western lives. We introduced ourselves to Sam, the gate guard, who gave us two parking permits and a map which we followed as we drove through the winding lanes to our unit. Russell had sent us the keys and as we approached the door to our new domicile I wondered if I should carry my wife across the threshold, but thought better of it because of my history of back problems. The front hedges were sparse and browned out, the first item on our list of to-do's. The mesquite tree had dropped debris all over the extra parking space and was pitched at a precarious angle to prohibit a car from pulling all the way forward. I hadn't noticed this on our Labor Day visit. This would be our second job. Why hadn't the landscapers of the home owners' association taken care of this? I had read the C.C. & R's.

I opened the door, half expecting to hear Spike and get ambushed by paint splatters, but it was quiet and light, lighter than I remembered. We inspected the kitchen, laundry room, proceeded into the living room. It seemed larger, more cavernous almost. We noticed the differences in the paint finish reflected by the sunlight and the stains on the berber rugs in both the back bedroom and the stairs leading up to the den. We poked into closets, checked cabinets, tested windows, faucets, toilets. In the space of fifteen minutes I could see all the things that had to be done. We had decided to lighten the ceilings, repaint the entire interior, redo the floors, change the cabinet handles and the light fixtures, fix up the back yard, replace the shrubs. I had brought my tape measure and pencil and pad, determined to organize these tasks logically. But where to begin? And the more we checked around, the more there needed to be done. Of course, being New Yorkers, we wanted it done yesterday. We had a week to get things in place because we figured if we could take care of some of this now, it would make it easier for us in the summer when we would move our remaining possessions. My wife couldn't wait to get going with the redecorating. It had been thirty years since we had bought furniture. It was going to be another adventure to fill this place…and expensive. But we had agreed on an amount of money to be spent…most coming from a retirement incentive I was to receive at the end of June. We figured we would have enough to do the place up right…and we wanted to make it comfortable…and classy…and ours.

Now all we had to do was find a painter, handy man, gardener, floor and floor man, doorman. We knew exactly one person in the entire state of Arizona, our realtor…and we had six days to arrange this. We had been thinking of little else for the past three months, not taking into account our house closing in New York, our jobs, and all the regular day to day aspects of being alive. Where did we begin? We had talked it over on the plane for the fifty thousandth time and knew that first would be the floor and then the painting. The other things would be done after these basics were completed. And they would be the dirtiest jobs so if we could get them going between April and July, we could proceed with the fun stuff when we got down here. Russell had assured us that he would help oversee the work. I think he felt guilty about the failure to get the rental.

We sat on the cold tile floor and were figuring where to start when there was a knock on the door. Our first visitor…who could it be?

A couple stared in at us, a tall, gray haired man, and his wife, a blond, strong looking woman. "Hello there. We're the Yorks, your neighbors. Two doors down. We saw your car and heard you were coming. Welcome."

"Oh, hi. Judy and Mike. Just got in from New York. Come on in." We followed them into the living room. "Sorry there's nowhere to sit."

"Oh, yeah!" A definite Canadian lilt, not like 'Oh, yeah,' in a challenging manner, but 'oh, yeah' in a 'I see' sort of confirmation. They looked around at the place. "This is just like Carl's unit. The up and down. Nice." They had definite accents.

"Carl?"

"Oh, yeah. Your next door neighbor. He's not here very often. He has the mirror version of your place. Uses it maybe a week a month."

"You live here all year?"

"No. Just six months. From Toronto. In fact, we're leaving at the end of the week. Just wanted to know if we could do anything for you?"

I felt like asking for everything. A telephone, maps, where the hardware stores were. The paint stores, rugs…if they knew anyone?

"Please feel free to use our telephone. And let us know…" They went on and we felt comfortable with this Canadian couple. They recommended that we speak to Sam the gate guard who knew everything and everyone who worked in the Casbah. They took us over to see their unit which they had bought from a friend after having rented it for two years. It was on one level, bright and airy, giving the illusion of spaciousness rather than the unusual levels and angles of our house. They gave us their yellow pages so we could research places to go. We arranged to go out to dinner with them on Tuesday. We had made our first friends in Arizona and we had good feelings about the Yorks

Later we walked around the gardens and went to Sam He gave us several cards for a handyman and painter named Roy who did a lot of work in the complex. He gave us directions to the nearest Home Depot and shopping centers. He told us of Teo, the landscaper and the chairman of the landscape committee to see about the tree. Sam was definitely the mayor of this place. I thanked him and hinted that if his recommendations worked out there would be something in it for him. He called me 'Sir." Things were perking and all within the first hour.

We found Roy working in an empty unit in the north section, installing a terra cotta floor. He was a lean, worn looking man, perhaps forty-five, tattooed on the forearm, smoking a cigarette as he worked, his face lined and craggy. His tee shirt was paint splattered and his jeans and work shoes dirty. He looked like a real workman! He stopped and walked us around the house, pointing out the shelves he had built, the bathroom tiles he had installed, the ceiling he had painted. "I love this place. Worked on at least ten places in here. Ask anyone about me. I'm fair and give you an honest job for the money." He talked to us for over half an hour. We were later to find that Roy was a gem of a man, skilled and hard working, but he loved to talk, smoke and drink coffee, three habits he indulged in as much as his work time on the job. But he was worth it just to hear his stories of his years in the navy and the gossip of many of the residents of the complex.

We noticed the saltillo tile floor was a weird pink color when the owner the the house, a woman in her thirties, introduced herself as Julie Altman. "Roy's terrific. He's fixing up the place cause we're getting ready to put it on the market. Don't want to move but my husband has to work in California and we just can't commute."

"We're thinking of a floor like yours. Want to make it white."

She giggled. "This wasn't supposed to be pink. It's a long story but my husband was here when the men came to color it. I was away on a trip. My husband's color blind. He picked this disgusting pink instead of the brown we wanted. I nearly killed him! Now it's going to be someone else's problem. We'll have no trouble selling the place, but I do feel embarrassed by the floor."

We told her about our experience and she recommended we go to the large furniture store near the Biltmore shopping center where her designer, a man named Michael O'Neill could be very helpful. Just mention her name. We thanked her and left with Roy.

We walked him over to our unit and he commented on the botched paint job. My wife walked him around pointing out the Arcadian doors she wanted replaced, the kitchen ceiling fixtures she wanted removed, the wood she wanted bleached out. "Sure is a nice place. We can make it look real nice." He was already using 'We' which was good. I wondered what he would charge. Roy made a list of all the improvements and jobs we wanted done. "I'll give you an estimate tomorrow. Be here in the morning." He could paint, do electrical work and plumbing. He didn't do doors but if we bought any kind of door handles, fixtures, wanted built ins…he did all that. When we told him our time frame, he said that would work out fine. We left him. But could we be this lucky so soon? And where could we get some other estimates. I called one painter from the yellow pages who would come over on Tuesday. I called the home insurance agent Russell had given to us and she seemed a friendly sort. She gave us the name of a contractor who also did the kinds of jobs we were looking for. His name was Carlson. We called him and he would come tomorrow evening. We used the York's telephone and arranged to have U.S. West, the telephone company to install a phone in our unit on Thursday. I already had an account an with Arizona Public Service for electricity.

We had been forewarned about scorpions and water bugs, alias roaches, so we got the name of an exterminator from Sam the gate guard. We left messages for Teo the gardener to call us at the hotel that night and went to the local eatery for lunch. We were starting and it felt good.

We went to the large furniture store near the restaurant and we drifted through, noticing how predominant neutral colors were and how large the pieces seemed to be. We introduced ourselves to Mike O'Neill who spotted us as Easterners in a second and of course had moved here from New Jersey ten years ago. He was helpful and gave us the name of a handyman and tile expert named Leo and the local jazz radio station. People were easy to talk to here and I continually had to curb my New York skepticism. He would come over in the afternoon tomorrow to give us some decorating ideas. The furniture and accessories in his store were extensive and expensive. We realized my bonus money was going to be easily spent. The cost of furniture had definitely gone up since the 1960's.

Leo, Mike's man, turned out to be a an old Italian gentleman who worked with his two sons. He owned a massive showroom featuring crude Mexican furnishings of every kind, floor coverings, fixtures, sinks…it was like a junkyard with a personality. We weren't sure whether to carpet the whole place or tile it. He pushed for stone. He showed us his stone cutting plant out back of his showroom. There were huge slabs of marble and granite as well as stocks of crates loaded with squares of every conceivable kind of stone imaginable. My wife knew she definitely wanted lighter floors. We had Italian terra cotta tiles in our New York home and loved them. She had the idea of using them and bleaching them white. The man showed us several samples but warned us that sometimes the Mexican saltillo, as he called them, tended to get bubble gum pinkish when whitewashed. If we wanted wood floors there were samples of different light colored woods. He called a customer and arranged for us to go look at a floor he had installed. He would come to measure tomorrow, if we wanted. We did.

The home he sent us to was magnificent, the woman coming from Chicago. She raved about the old man and his sons. It was a nice floor. We never liked wood before, but it was something to think about. We thanked her. We checked around and went into two other floor places we found in the area. One warned us not to get wood. The heat made the floors buckle and the white saltillo often wore in heavy trafficked areas. This one guy offered to come and measure for carpeting. We told him we were on a tight time schedule and probably wouldn't want the work done until July. It didn't matter. He would come tomorrow afternoon.

We found furniture stores in several places, two home depots, a window store. We spent all afternoon looking at floors, paints, doors for the living room. French doors were going to replace the sliding Arcadian doors. The big dilemma was what to do with the floors? Should we go with wood, or saltillo? Leo pushed for granite which was the most expensive, of course.

We went to several house models late in the afternoon and saw several types of ceramic floors. One had stone, a light colored marble, and another had something called travertine. Lime stone and flagstone were used in several. One was nicer than the rest and we finished the day by going to Arizona Tile, an institution in the Valley and getting a lesson in types of stone and ceramic floors. The prices were amazingly high and that didn't include labor.

The more we saw the more confused we got. And we wanted to make a choice soon. It was only the end of the first day and we were perking, but our energies were wandering in all directions. We got back to our hotel room that night, tired, excited and confused.

9

Easter vacation?

The next three days were a whirlwind of meetings, estimates, decisions. It was worse than work! Roy's written proposal was for $2,000. It included paint, electrical work and other minor plumbing repairs. Two other painters came in over $3,000 without paint. Roy even gave us paint samples. He seemed to know his stuff but was he too cheap? I liked him and would have given him the O.K. on the spot, less bother and we have personal references…but it couldn't be that quick and easy. Was I crazy or had a lifetime of being bamboozled colored my judgement? So we tortured ourselves until the last Sunday when we forked over $1,000 to him, set a time schedule for July 2 and felt relieved, both emotionally and financially! He said it would take two weeks to do the place. Sounded good!

We made our first Arizona purchase of two plastic lawn chairs so we didn't have to sit on the floor while waiting for all the potential tradesmen to come. It took us a half-hour in an Osco Drug Store to decide between white and green, as if it really mattered. This would be the easiest decision we would have to make all year! Here we had a house but couldn't use it. It's more fun to spend $150 a night at a hotel. Why sleep on the floor? Thirty years ago we would have. The $1,000 saved could have gone for a piece of furniture or wall paper or paint or…but what the hell, we were getting a free corn flake breakfast and Sanka…it went on and on!

Michael O'Neill came over that Sunday and spent two hours with my wife, sketching out rooms, suggesting colors, furniture placement, light angles. He was into some Oriental philosophy of space called Feng Shui (phonetic spelling, pardon me). The big challenge was where to position the bed, which we didn't own yet, having sold our set at the infamous yard sale last March, in the master bedroom. I tired of this enigma and spent time checking plumbing, appliances and meeting Tio the gardener. Michael, although married and a father, had a feminine nature which I found irritating, so I let my wife deal with him. We had commented on his appearance upon our earlier meeting. He wore black lizard western boots with silver tips, white jeans, a crinkled white dress shirt, red plaid vest and tie printed with horses and pineapple. It made quite a statement; maybe he was related to a Philippino jockey! But he was a 'designer.' I called him a decorator but he corrected me immediately. Pardon me! I guess we could excuse his eccentric attire, earring and stubble cheeks. He 'adored' us because we came from New York City. I wondered what his house was like and his family. I could only speculate. He was going to be disappointed when we wouldn't purchase a lot from his store, but let the designer beware! My wife had a good sense of style, far different from his. He was extreme, favoring black and gold, the bed angled diagonally out from a corner, a television suspended by wires from the ceiling. It sounded like a set from a porno movie. He sensed my displeasure and blew me off as a male clod. Fine with me. I had real work to do.

I met another resident, a young gay man who was chairman of the landscape committee of the Casbah. Clifford listened to my wish to take out the mesquite tree in front. He was polite and told me he would consult the board of managers on Monday and get back to me. He later had us over for coffee. His apartment looked like a Bloomingdale's designer showcase room—antiques, classic paintings, green walls, swords, English pottery—in fact it had been featured in "Phoenix Home and Garden" magazine. I was beginning to learn that Phoenicians weren't tobacco chewing cowboys, but people as diverse as those we knew back East. Clifford favored Ralph Lauren clothes, while his 'friend' Frederick was an Izod advocate…He was athletic and masculine. We liked this couple and by the end of our visit Clifford told me to remove the tree, just replace it with other shrubs. "No one has to know," he confided in me. So much for C,C & R's! Clifford also endorsed Roy, warning us to stay out of his way or he would waste half the day bullshitting and the job would take twice as long.

Tio took $200 to remove both mesquite trees, front and back, and would do it after we left. Cash in hand, no receipt. Teo was a small Mexican, smiling and polite, driving an old brown Chevy pick up loaded with garden tools, a five gallon water jug, and two teenage boys who were his 'cousins' he said. He was the only one of the three who spoke English. The boys just smiled under their soiled baseball caps. Was I becoming an employer of illegal aliens?

The insurance agent's reference, a contractor named Carlson, referred us to a wallpaper man, his cousin Brad, and a door man, his cousin Chuck. Everyone had cousins in this state! We had Roy so Carlson lost out on the other work. He didn't seem to mind. Both relatives showed up and we got an estimate on papering three bathrooms at $17 a roll and stripping off the old for an additional $200. We considered that excessive, but I had painted and papered our old house twice, broke my back, and my wife pledged I would never be asked to do it again, one of the great concessions in my life, the other being that I didn't have to take out the garbage anymore. It would be worth every penny to watch him work!

The Arcadian doors could be replaced with French doors, if you please, three units. We debated for three days whether to have single panes or six glass panels on each door, finally deciding on single pane to lighten up the place. We selected from brochures, hoping they were of good quality, as if we would know the difference until we lived with them and they might blow open in a stiff wind. Chuck would choose the brass hardware and have them in by the time we came down in July.

He took half the money required and would get the rest when we arrived. Boy, I was giving out money right and left. And most of the work would be done while we would be back in New York. In God we trust…and in Roy, Brad and Chuck too!

The big issue of the floors was still unresolved as of Friday. We voted out wood, which suited a New York City apartment. We liked saltillo white but the quality and color of the Mexican tile was inferior and Leo gave us an estimate of $11,000 not including jack hammering out the old tiles. He was a stubborn old cuss and wouldn't bargain. He was the first local I felt uneasy about.

The second estimate was for $10,000. Finally, we were sent by Michael O'Neill to a stone distributor in Tempe. Not only didn't I know where this place was, but I mispronounced the name with a silent 'e' until corrected at a gas station. We were directed down a highway called the Hohokum Expressway, allegedly named for an ancient Indian tribe, ended up in an industrial park south of the airport…lost. We accidentally discovered a silk tree company, two furniture outlets but not the stone warehouse. By surprise we discovered a huge Asian enclave here. Orientals were everywhere and we wondered if we had stumbled upon an illegal immigrant colony. We later learned that large computer companies were located in the area. Several young men were on their lunch break but none spoke English well. Finally one young engineer directed us to our destination. He was the only one who spoke something other than math and computerese. The good to come out of this was that if there were this many Asians in Phoenix, there must be some good Chinese restaurants. Being a New Yorker I had to have my weekly fix of won ton soup, egg rolls and moo shu pork.

We met a wonderful Nebraskan named Tim Reilly who ran the huge stone establishment. He toured us around and spent two hours explaining granite, marble and ceramic floors even though we were a small time customer. He seemed to enjoy it and so did we. Live and learn. We had lunch with him and he convinced us to use travertine. He was a hell of a nice guy, slow, sure of himself and reassuring. He understood our situation. We deposited $2,000 toward a $4,000 order. He set the cases of stone aside and promised to hold them until our workman came to pick them up. He swore it was an extraordinary lot. We absolutely trusted Tim. He had family photographs on his desk, a Cornhusker banner on the wall and told us of his visit to New York City in 1955 when his car was impounded.

Tim knew of Leo and reinforced our bad vibes about him. He gave us the name of Stan Tish to call. "He lives on my block and is a great tile man." So we owned stone now too! Tim made me promise to have him over for beer when the New York Giants played the Cardinals in October. It was a deal. We left with 2 heavy sample pieces which we took on the plane back with us to New York and which my wife made me lug around everytime we went shopping for furniture, towels and fabric. They conveniently fit in my attache case. I felt like a depression era gangster lugging a tommy gun around in a violin case! I carried this 16x16 slab all over Manhattan. Boy, did I build up my arm strength over the next two months.

Stan the tile man couldn't be reached over the weekend so we left Phoenix with a painter, door man, wall paperer, gardener, several new acquaintances, 800 square feet of travertine, but no one to install it. Leo was out. We told him so and he grudgingly accepted the rejection.

The week we got back to New York my wife called Stan at 5 P.M. our time, 3 P.M. his. He was still out on a job. He must be a good worker, or slow. His wife was lovely and won us over. She was a cake caterer from Iowa originally and she and Stan had moved to the valley ten years ago. He used to install floors for Dillards in the Midwest and now free lanced. She told us he was an artist.

The next night Stan called us and we liked him immediately. He had spoken to Tim Reilly, gave us a price which brought the job in at $8,500 and worked out a schedule to take out the old floor at the end of June and install the new in early July. He made us feel comfortable about the job. It's funny how one adjusts. $8,500 seemed a bargain now. It took me two months to make that kind of money and here I was only too glad to pay it out for a floor, for God's sake. I had come a long way since my days growing up in Brooklyn.

10

Leaving New York with a bang

The period between Easter and June 26th, the last day of school, was filled with nightly phone calls to Stan the tile man, Chuck the door man, Sam the gate guard and Russell. It got to be a habit to hear Russell's Virginia drawl every night at eleven telling us about all the goings on at the Casbah. He was our 'Tonight' show. The trees had been removed and the yard cleaned up by Teo and his cousins. The French doors were installed but the old ones were leaning against the outside patio wall. Chuck told us they were too heavy for him to haul off and he thought maybe someone in the complex would use them. I didn't argue. The travertine was in crates in the carport covered by a tarpaulin. Stan would start to work in late June as soon as he finished the job he was on. We had informed Sam the gate guard of this and sent him a present— $20. He was our friend for life, or until Christmas bonus time. Mrs. Tish promised us a cake on our arrival. She was a honey. We kept in touch with Roy too and his phone calls were always the most expensive. Clifford was right; he could really talk.

Our plan was to go into school the last Friday of June, pick up our checks, deliver our second car to a teacher in my wife's school who had bought it and then drive to the airport for a 6 P.M. flight to Phoenix. Our newer car was transported the previous Monday with a promise it would be waiting for us when we arrived. The movers had taken what little furniture we had left on Thursday, leaving us to sleep on the floor of our empty apartment that last night. We would carry three suitcases of clothes and personal belongings plus my 16x16 travertine tile. I sort of got to like it and thought about chipping off a piece and wearing it on a chain around my neck. It was a symbol of the financial burden I carried. I was so attached to our new floor.   We would live in a cheap motel the first week of July. Our plan was to have the master bed and bathroom painted first and we would then move in and live in this back area while Roy and Stan did their thing in the rest of the house. We could shop for furnishings, rugs and hopefully have the place done by the end of July.

Ah, the best laid schemes. That last day did 'gang agley.' At 7:30 A.M. we were on our way. My wife would drop me off at my school. I would get my last pay check and bonus, say my good byes and wait for her to pick me up in the afternoon. My wife would go to her school for pay and farewells and turn the car over to the buyer who had agreed to take us to Kennedy airport. It would go like clockwork.

Then 'bang!' literally, as we drove along Jericho Turnpike. I knew the muffler had blown and my 1987 Camry sounded like a 1936 Messerschmitt! Oh, God. We couldn't deliver the car like this. I had changed the oil, filters, tuned it, gassed it up and washed my old reliable Toyota…and now she was letting me down. The buyer had even paid us for the car in cash on Wednesday. Thinking fast I cowardly let my wife drop me off (I was due in at 7:30, she at 8), as I ordered her to get to Speedy Muffler King and beg them to help us out. I knew they opened early. I prayed that meant 7 A.M. not 9!

I learned later that my wife deserved an Oscar for her performance that morning. The shop actually opened at 8 but at 7:40 when the manager saw or heard her drive up, he opened the door and saw her face. He didn't say anything, but "pull it into bay 1." She told me she had tears streaming down her cheeks and smoke coming out of her ears, quite a contradiction in emotions. She sobbed and growled her tale of woe and

Mr. Speedy lived up to his name and had the muffler replaced in ten minutes for only $19.95, the advertised price. I think it's the first time in automotive history that a customer was not gouged for the price of clamps, three sections of tail pipe, screws, nuts, bolts and coffee for the mechanic on his inevitable work break in the middle of his speedy job.

She laughed as she told me the story on the plane, but it wasn't funny at the time. I excused my bail out by claiming the job would never have been done if a man had brought the car in. My power of persuasion ran to cursing and hard stares, not the pathetic helplessness of my Meryl Streep! I'm sure in the future we'll tell and retell this story again and again, with pleasure, but at the time it was unbelievable, something that only happened in a Three Stooge's comedy, Nyuk, Nyuk, Nyuk! It's like a nightmare vision I used to have when house painting, of dropping an open can of paint on the living room rug.

So, we left New York, not with a sigh and a whisper, but with a bang, hopefully not to crash in the desert like a Phoenix, in Phoenix!

11

White paint, beige carpets and wall paper too!

During our first week in Scottsdale we stayed in a downtown motel, five minutes from the Casbah. It was the July 4th weekend, the first holiday we would fail to acknowledge in my retirement which we hoped would be 365 holidays a year. All days are the same to a retiree, hopefully each one special. The temperatures reached 112 degrees and we were surprised the motel was filled. We learned that Europeans from Italy and France were prolific during the summer, no doubt hornswaggled into touring the desert in summer by some enterprising travel agents in Rome and Paris. As Mark Twain said, 'the innocents ain't all abroad.'

We were anxious to get into our new home but first we had to surmount several obstacles, namely selecting a paint color and getting the master bedroom painted as well as the bathroom ceilings so that Brad could paper. We met Stan Tish and after speaking to him continually by phone all spring, we were anxious to see him face to face. Stan was short and squat, built like a baseball catcher perhaps from working on his hands and knees for hours at a time. He was perhaps 35 years of age, with an Irish ruddy complexion, long blond hair and mischievous sparkling blue eyes. We were on intimate terms with him within minutes, especially when he presented us with a beautiful, 10 inch high chocolate layer cake his wife made for us which we devoured with our fingers at 8:30 A.M. using paper towels for napkins. Our furnishings weren't to arrive until the following weekend. As we wiped chocolate fudge off our faces, Stan showed us the floor, now stripped down to its concrete base, and explained his work plan. His tools and tile saw were set up in the atrium, formerly Spike's kennel. He had moved some of the travertine there also, along with bags of cement compound stacked along the exterior house wall. He loved the stone, showing us the grain running in several pieces, explaining that Tim Reilly had done well by us in his selection. Stan's helper was coming tomorrow and they would start laying the floor from the front door and hallway back to the living room branching out from there. He had met Roy last week and the two men had worked it out so Stan could lay tiles while Roy painted the ceilings in other areas and then the walls throughout. It might be a bit crowded but they would get the job done for us. "How long?" we asked.

"A few weeks. Don't worry. It's going to look sensational."

It was hard for us to believe. There were chips of red saltillo scattered about and dust everywhere. It coated the walls, counter tops, cabinets…It was a 'smog' we would come to endure during the next month and a half. The two week deadline didn't quite work!

We told Stan our intention to meet the mover on Saturday and live in the rear of the house. He assured us it would be no problem.

Roy showed up next and said he could get started as soon as we chose the paint and color.

Then the doorbell rang and in pranced Michael O'Neill, on his way to work, wearing his boots, a redneck bandanna, and his white jeans. He wanted us to come by the store to see a bed he just knew was perfect for us. He noticed our paint samples and suggested white, not too stark, but Dunn Edwards definitely. He was very dramatic in his recommendations. "We must get our palette settled, now mustn't we." I caught Roy and Stan smirking at each other in acknowledgement of Michael's 'artistic demeanor'. We introduced the two to Michael who excused himself with a 'Ta, ta. Until later.'

Stan, Roy and I bonded immediately in laughter and my wife gently chided them explaining his role in our plans. Roy was the more diplomatic of the two and promised not to make fun of Michael's 'temperament.' Stan then granted the designer his new sobriquet, a nickname we still use to this day when referring to Mr. O'Neill. 'Mikey White Pants.' It marked the start of a positive relationship for all of us. Kind of a common enemy to unify against…but he wasn't really our enemy and ultimately proved useful to a degree.

We sat down with Roy and studied white paint chips. He would dilute the paint with 50% water to whitewash the ceilings and then spray the rest of the house.

"How long?"

"Oh, about a week." This seemed to be a standard answer. For the next hour we debated the myriad varieties of white paint.

Now I always thought in terms of white as a symbol of virginity, the purity of brides, peace, goodness, clean as in hospitals, surrender with a white flag, the white knight on the white horse, the white tornado, white bread, white rice, the home team, Whitey Ford (my boyhood Yankee idol), even white lies. There is of course a white Christmas, the white cliffs of Dover, the White House, the great White Way, "don't shoot till you see the whites of their eyes!" But when it came time to painting the walls of my house, I learned to look at white in a new light…or rather in many new lights. What could be so hard as picking up a few cans of white paint? Our next stop was the paint store. Was I naive. There I discovered a stock of a dozen varieties of whites: bisque, sterling silver, Navajo white, pearl white, Swiss coffee, dawn, bone, Celtic linen, cottage white, chalky, alabaster and lily. Everything but seasick pallor! I can picture the copywriters sitting around a table going berserk to think of these names. I imagine automobile people have the same problem when thinking of names for the colors of their paint finishes on the new models. Now to me Swiss coffee is brown. Celtic linen involves green. Sterling silver is, well, metallic. Dawn is pink. I found out differently. And you can be thrown off by the light in which you view the color sample cards. The stores all have fluorescent lighting which differs from regular electric light bulbs, which in turn differ from sun light and there are also changes with different angles of the sun at different times of the day. So we took home sample cards and pasted them up on the walls. They were of course too small to really judge and we brought them back to be told that the sample cards often are darker than the actual paint. So how do we surmount this problem? We bought four quarts of the paints which appealed to us, brought them home and painted splotches on the walls of different rooms. This cost us approximately $30. I couldn't tell the difference before my wife decided none of them was right. I was snow blind! Cottage white was too yellow, bone too stark. Swiss coffee was too tan and Navajo white was too brown. I was baffled. Wasn't there just plain old house white, the vanilla white of ice cream? No. That's too sterile. So we went back to the paint emporium (not called a store in these modern times). The oft repeated and recurring comment which I have grown to love and adore from my wife was, "I'll know it when I see it?"

Lo and behold I found there were variations of each of these four basic whites. And each card had five shadings of each variant. Oh joy! Of course the only way to test these was again to take home a small amount to try on the wall. This time we narrowed it down to bone china and willowy white which cost us another $16. I had run out of brushes by this time so that was another $10. Plus gas for the car.

But this wasn't the end of it. We had to decide on the consistency of the paint. Should we get the paint in flat, low sheen, eggshell, semi-gloss or gloss? The store expert recommended eggshell so I grudgingly acceded. By now I was downright stubborn in accepting anything from these guys. So back we went to the house and painted big patches of each. I sarcastically suggested we paint the place in alternating stripes of each hue. No good! We decided on 'bone china' after asking Sam the gate guard, Clifford and Frederick and two handymen who happened to be sweeping the walks just outside our front door. Who knows why these men were more adept as color experts than I? I liked bone china right away but that wasn't good enough for the wife. So we did the neighborhood survey and reached a consensus.

I figured I was home free but I was wrong. Now in New York the best paint you can buy is Benjamin Moore. In Arizona it's Dunn Edwards or, according to Roy, Home Depot's Behr, which is less expensive. But why save money? So before we bought the Dunn Edwards we found the one dealer who did actually import Benjamin Moore. The place was about five miles the other side of the Valley. Of course we went. I remember painting my mother's house thirty years ago. We picked the paint color at 8 A.M. bought the paint a half-hour later and had the place finished by 4 P.M. What happened to those days of yesteryear when men were men and white paint was white paint? Benjamin Moore's variety of colors corresponded with Dunn Edwards, just different names. I couldn't tolerate any more samples, splotch painting, not to mention excursions to every paint store in Phoenix, Scottsdale, Mesa, Gilbert and Glendale. It took me twenty minutes to find the paint department in the Home Depot, a store roughly the size of Nebraska. Jokingly I suggested we use our airline tickets to take a quick six hour shuttle back to New York City to buy the stuff back at Aboff's Paint Store in Smithtown, Long Island, our old home town. My wife didn't take kindly to that and I had an afternoon of frozen glares and no talking.

It took 2 days for Roy to spray the bed room and ceilings with bone china and after breathing in the stuff daily and wiping it off every surface in the house, I learned to like it. If I had gone for a chest x-ray I'm sure my lungs would have that color show up. I wonder if the technician would know what tint we used?

So, that's what I learned about white. I promise myself never to have to do this again. I hope the paint stays on for the rest of my lifetime.

Now that the stuff is on, I do admit it does look good and I suppose worth the angst!

But my ordeal was not over. Now I'm told we have to pick beige carpet which will blend with the walls. We went over to the local carpet store and approached the eager, smiling salesman. "We're interested in beige carpets."

"Beige?" he responded as he took out a huge sample portfolio and opened it to two dozen two inch swatches pasted across the cardboard. "Now which shade of beige pleases you?"

'My God!" I thought. "It's another white paint fiasco!" I must have turned ashen white…like a ghost!

It all began again. We brought home carpet sample books, each weighing at least 20 pounds. Between the travertine and the paint and carpet samples I was broadening my chest and arms by inches. Next my shirts wouldn't fit and I would have to spring for a new supply. Maybe I would save money by not joining a health club.

I learned about weaves, piles, wool as opposed to synthetic fibers, twists, shags, velvets…We had the same multiplicity of shadings and exotic names before finally settling on a beige oak color from a California mill which could be delivered and installed in four weeks. So we left a deposit, figured we'd have the floor and walls done by the end of July and then could fill the place up with furniture and accessories. I couldn't wait to start spending that retirement incentive money.

Mikey White Pants' bed turned out to be a bronze gold iron frame, decorated with two large curlicues composing the head and foot boards which we liked immediately. The cost was an astounding $2500, sans mattress and spring. We wanted to purchase it, but I would have nightmares paying that much to sleep. We would give it more thought, a euphemism for 'no way, Jose.' But we didn't give up. Mikey gave us a Polaroid photo of the bed and an article from his bible, 'Architectural Digest' with a story on the designer. The frame was called 'Ocean Wave.' I joked that it must be for a water bed but the only thing that was getting me sea sick was the price. The next day while hiding out in our back bedroom as Roy, masked like a surgeon sprayed the ceiling…and us…we considered springing for the bed. Clifford came by and saved us $1,000. He knew an ironworker in Mesa who could make anything in metal at reasonable prices. He telephoned for us and made an appointment with Karl for that afternoon.

We found the foundry, a large workshop complete with anvils and furnaces and showed Karl the picture. He was a taciturn man who spoke monosyllabically but had a solid, stabile presence. He could make the bed in two weeks (what else?) and color it any shade we wanted. No money down, cash on delivery. We shook hands on it, felt wonderful about saving $1,000, and sweated about breaking the news to Mikey White Pants.

We ended up buying fabric for bedding from him, at an inflated price, to justify his time with us and appease our guilt.

Brad, the wallpaper man, came the next day and took two minutes to strip the paper off the front bathroom walls. This was for $200! I debated with him but got nowhere. He was stubborn and in order to get him to continue the job, I left the issue alone. Roy and Stan overheard the argument and later in the day confided in me that they didn't like the guy.

Brad needed one more day to finish the job and I engaged him in sports talk to soften him up. He was an Arizona Cardinals fan and I told him that his team could never win with their quarterbacks, Boomer Esiason from my long suffering New York Jets, and Kent Graham, a second rate backup who used to be with my beloved New York Giants, who play in New Jersey, pardon me! It's a New York thing!

Instead of drawing us together, this alienated Brad more and when he finished the job, which looked damned good, I presented him with a check $150 less than our agreed upon price saying his charge for stripping was unfair, unreasonable and a rip off. He made a face and complained about the difficulty in papering the 'soft' walls with their curves and irregularities. Roy and Stan showed up behind me, all of a sudden. I realized it was for support in case there was trouble and Brad reluctantly accepted the check and left without a goodbye.

"He ain't a happy camper, but he won't be back. Not if he knows what's good for him," Stan declared.

"I hope the stuff doesn't unpeal tonight," I joked.

Roy assured me that despite Brad's surliness, the papering was done well. So in three days we had the bathrooms wall papered, the master bedroom painted, a length of travertine floor laid from the front door to the living room, a carpet and bed ordered, and a mild case of white lung disease.

We were perking!

12

First night. Water, water everywhere!

We still hadn't stayed overnight in our house and were anxious to get out of the motel, unpack our bags, use our own furnishings and have a home cooked meal. It finally happened on Saturday.

The movers unloaded the truck in the morning. Our kitchen set was shifted into the master bedroom, our mattress and spring which would go into the guest room once we bought a new one for our "Ocean Wave" knock off and 44 cartons of books, phonograph records (yes, I have 500 great jazz, show, pop and classical albums from the 50;s—80's which I refuse to throw out or sell. I have nursed my turntable along for 30 years and hope to keep it until death do us part, its or mine!), pots, pans, dishes, sheets, towels. There were also a few winter clothes which we would keep for return vacations to New York. There was my word processor and important documents. All items were placed in the center of the carpeted rooms under sheets for protection from the 'white clouds' of Roy's paint sprayer. We also found a headboard which didn't belong to us. We informed the mover's head office in Fort Wayne, Indiana (remember the Fort Wayne Zoellner Pistons you N.B.A. fans over the age of 50?). It took them two weeks to pick it up. I wonder what the owners were going through, not that it looked very valuable. I also wonder if people would have done the same for me? I hope so!

During the week several neighbors stopped by out of kindness and curiosity. We had drinks with several of them and showed everyone the house 'in progress.' Several reciprocated and we toured other homes and were impressed with them, especially those in our phase. It was interesting to see the variety of tastes and styles running from American traditional to Southwestern turquoise and pink. One had marvelous Moroccan decor and another, the most comical, had a golf motif from racks of golf balls to a display of visors and hats from courses all over the world. The place was a Van's golf shop residence. Pictures of famous fairways and greens covered the walls. Even the carpet had a golf theme. The owner of this home, Jim Grogan, was an Alabaman who married May, an English woman from Manchester. They were retired, made a fortune from Amway, and vowed to play all 191 golf courses in the Valley. At the rate they were being built, I didn't know if they would succeed. It surprised us that he had made money in Amway. In New York City it was considered a joke. You could buy anything in the Big Apple and didn't need mail order and pyramid schemes...but we were to learn, New York isn't America. Jim still traveled as a motivational speaker for the company conventions, all expenses paid. Maybe he could motivate Roy and Stan to get done faster!

We met Margie, an elderly Waspish lady who inherited her father's fortune and only lived here for two months a year. She was very severe and intimidated us. She had a beautiful garden.

There was an unusual couple, the Chesters, who always wore matching shirts. We went to dinner with them at a cheap restaurant that didn't have air conditioning. We didn't know any better! He liked to be called J.P. His wife was P.J. It was like Tweedledum and Tweedledee. When we talked, the price of everything was the key. J.P. was into thrift in a big way. "Buy your plants at Tip Top Nursery. They have a two for one on geraniums. Shop at Costco. They have a special on toilet paper. Pizza on 68th Street is only $8.95 for a large..." It went on and on like this all evening, even to his telling us how to economize on air conditioning and hot water.

Still another neighbor, from Bermuda, invited us to play tennis. They owned an inn on that island and vacationed here in winter. Jane was a large woman, at least 250 pounds, who dug herself in at the net, immovable, and hit everything back she could reach, which wasn't very much. She wore whites, long tights and long sleeves, no skin exposed whatsoever, except her face which was difficult to see under her visor. She was a real tennis 'mummy.' Her husband, Geoff, was a good deal older than she and genuinely loved to play, but his reflexes had slowed making it difficult for us not to lose a point. Being the gentleman that I am, I let them stay in the set until the end when I blasted one off Jane's ample belly. The game ended amicably and we discovered they were more interested in martinis after the tennis than the game itself. Joan was 'veddy' British.

The domed mosque was occupied on weekends by David Speer, who wrote and produced a leading television sitcom. He was very private, but it was reported to us by Clifford that he threw wild parties. People spied into his home when he wasn't there through a large window. He had put over one quarter million dollars into renovating the place and it was magnificent. Several television actors, his guests, were seen at the big swimming pool on weekends.

On the whole it was a promising beginning. The neighbors were as varied and unique as we had hoped

To get back to more practical matters, when the movers left, my wife was determined to cook a meal so she tried the stove. It worked. All the appliances were top quality. Being a man, I read through the manuals we found in a kitchen drawer. My wife plunged right in…and overcooked the sauce for the pasta, but it was still delicious. Our dishes made the place seem like home. Forget the fact that we ate on a kitchen table in the back bedroom. It was our kitchen table.

Our first mishap occurred after dinner with the dishwasher. It had a panel of buttons and lights that looked like the controls on a 747. My wife figured out what to do and we started the machine, half expecting it to take off. Ouila! It worked!

But ten minutes later I heard a scream. "Come here, fast!" I raced to the kitchen to find soap bubbles frothing out of the washer door. "Oh, Oh!" It was a scene from "Mr. Roberts" when Ensign Pulver blew up the ship's laundry. It was funny but not at the moment. I opened the door to discover a solid block of suds. What to do? Why did it happen? Check the book? No luck. So we called J.P. who came over. I hoped he wouldn't recommend that it would be cheaper to wash the dishes by hand.

As it turned out, my wife had used manual sink dishwashing fluid instead of machine detergent. It was nice of P.J. or J.P. (I was getting them mixed up now) to come over to help but it made us feel like morons…"Duh, we're the dummies from New York."

So we pulled the suds out by hand, ran the rinse cycle three times before the soap dissipated and had our first lesson in using the appliances. My wife vowed to read all the manuals in the morning.

The shower worked fine although the hot water heater located in a back yard storage closet chugged a bit. I hoped it was from disuse. The next day Roy showed me how to adjust the water temperature and when I showered the water scalded me, so I guess it was working fine.

Water was a major problem in the Valley. It was hard and full of calcium and other corrosive minerals. When you washed anything, be it a glass or car, it left a cloudy film. It was what we old timers from Brooklyn call 'Flatbush Water." The City of New York had done away with that fifty years ago, but not Phoenix. During the following week, upon advice of neighbors, we learned about reverse osmosis and water softening. As it turned out, we had an R.O. system (I was learning the lingo) installed in the kitchen for the drinking water and refrigerator, but to install a water softener would entail two large storage tanks to be stationed at the main water intake valve located right next to our front door in the car port. This would be an eye sore and a no-no according to the C.C. & R.'s. You know, it compromises the 'architectural integrity' of the Casbah. I didn't want tanks there either. This was not a trailer camp! The only way to install a system was to put the tanks at the rear of the house and run copper pipes up the front wall, across the roof and down the back. It would cost over $2500 instead of the $1000 for the system. So we only got the R.O. and saved the $2500. So what if we would have lizard skin and stiff laundry? We could buy a lot of skin moisturizers for the money!

I was looking forward to a good night's sleep on my own mattress after suffering at the motel on a too short, too soft bed. Our own sheets and pillows felt familiar although the room was strange and disorient-ing. It would take time to feel at home here, but my body liked the old mattress. I was tired from unpacking, breathing dust, bailing out the dishwasher and feeling humiliated. I needed sleep and was enjoying the notion of sleeping late on Sunday. Stan and Roy were taking off and we could stash away some of our belongings. The ZZZ's came easily.

Sometime later, in the darkness, and I have never experienced black like desert night black, I thought I heard rain. I must be imagining it. But no, there was definitely water hitting the building. We got up and as I stared outside, I swore there was water sprinkling up from the ground in several places. I groaned, cursed and slipped on a pair of shorts, stepped outside the French doors to tip toe along the pathway to the backyard. Of course I banged my knee on Stan's wet saw. In my imagi-nation, fed by tales of scorpions, tarantulas and rattlesnakes in Arizona, I was expecting to be attacked by hoards of wild, night creatures. Instead I was splattered from all sides by water gushing out of the soaker system whose controlling heads had been knocked off. The water sprinklers were on a timer , I later learned, and went off on Monday, Wednesday and Friday from 5 to 6 A.M. They were supposed to drip…obviously they didn't! Instead they shot water straight up, about face high. I felt like a car in a car wash tunnel. I might be the first

Arizonan to drown in his own backyard…without falling into a pool! I finally groped around, found the metal control box and pressed the 'off' button. As I wiped the water from my face I saw the largest brown cockroach of all time perched on top of the box. I jumped back, looked around for more, could see nothing, and hot footed it back inside.

I dried off, checked for bugs, got back into bed, and wondered if moving here was such a good idea. I knew if I told the wife about the roach, a.k.a. water bug, desert beetle, Palmetto bug, the house would be up for sale in the morning.

But we did survive our first night…and managed to control a new set of machines, both inside and out. I always had been told water was the key problem in the desert. I learned the truth of this the hard way!

13

Two weeks = two months

By the second week we realized Stan and his helper Don would need at least a month to finish laying the travertine. Stan was meticulous in his cutting and laying the stone. He had finished the entryway and hall and had a row of tiles into the living room, but there was still the kitchen, laundry and dining area to complete. Stan groaned on his stiff knees and showed us how tightly he laid the tiles. He said we would be able to skim a coin over the floor when he finished without any interference, bump free. Stan came to work early and left early. His hours were 7 A.M. to 3 P.M. and we had no objection, but the work went slowly and he wasn't being paid by the hour or day. I figured that what he made from this job was not going to make him a millionaire, but he was a real craftsman, often matching the grain on the stone to insure a unified look. The outside atrium was white with spray from the saw, chips from the stone and splash from the mud compound mixing. The green plants looked as if they had been sprayed with snow crystals for Christmas, but it was July in the heat. Don, the helper, was a jovial guy who enjoyed sweets and Pepsi which we supplied daily to keep him happy. We must have bought a gross of chocolate chip cookies from the bakery at A.J.'s and gallons of soda. Don, we figured, must have very bad teeth and high dental bills.

Roy was almost done with the painting, except for the cabinet and closet doors, which he had removed to sand down and paint at the workshop at his house. He had removed all the hardware, knobs and cabinet pulls (there were 50) and my wife decided to buy new ones anyway, a chore which became another adventure. With no doors, paint spray residue invaded the insides of the closets and required daily cleaning. We finally gave up and decided to wait until the job was done. It was a losing battle against the white smog.

The two eight by four foot sliding Arcadian doors left by Chuck the door man had to be disposed of since no one wanted them. The dumpster was 100 yards away. Roy and I carried one and Stan and Don the other. The damned things weighed over 100 pounds apiece and the edges cut into my hands. The effort to move the cumbersome doors hurt and we all covered up our discomfort with jokes. The strain was overwhelming but male pride kept me from hollering 'uncle.' My back and shoulders were crying for relief. This was a job for a younger man but we managed to get to the dumpster to find they were too large to fit inside so we left them along side. I joked about getting a hernia, standard line for heavy lifting. I found out a month later that I was a prophet when I discovered an unnatural protrusion poking out of my lower abdomen. But that's for a later chapter.

As it turned out, Sam the gate guard telephoned to say we couldn't leave the doors there. The garbage company wouldn't take anything not inside the dumpster. One of the neighbors had turned me in. That afternoon I called several private carters but none would do a job that small. Finally Sam came through again. For $10 he got the Casbah landscapers to throw the doors on their truck. Money talks! God knows where they ended up but don't be surprised to see them for sale at some local's yard sale.

Choosing cabinet handles also turned out to be an experience similar to choosing paint and carpet. The wife wanted different pulls for each room. The kitchen would match the chrome trim on the appliances.

The bathrooms would each be different and the dining room would depend on the ceiling fixture we would eventually purchase.

With our gang of workers busy with their tasks, ours days were spent shopping, ferreting out all those items we needed. Even though we had no dining room set, we found a wonderful copper gold chandelier at the Iron Mart which Roy would hang for us. "Ain't no big deal," he proclaimed.

We also got rid of three kitchen ceiling fixtures which looked like tomato cans. We bought three modern Italian halogen lights which hung down three feet from the fifteen foot ceiling. "Ain't no big deal," Roy repeated. "I'll take care of them when I get the doors done."

We took a sample of the chandelier color to Home Depot at the Pavilions, to get twelve cabinet pulls for the dining room. We found some we liked but they only had ten. The clerk called their other stores on Bell Road and Thomas until he tracked down two others. He did and we learned our way around two new areas as we drove madly to Home Depot 2. We got other handles for one bathroom at the Thomas Road store and the other two bathrooms back at the Pavilions. The kitchen required our taking home three different handles from each branch and trying them out.

Again we got a consensus from Stan, Don, Roy, Clifford, Frederick, P.J. and J.P. Only Sam was missing. By a vote of six to two, Frederick and I were voted down, we chose heavy silver pulls with shell scrolls decorating the ends. Why the sea shell decor in the desert puzzled me but I was beyond asking now. Just get the darn things up already.

Of course the other two handles had to be returned, which amazingly was no problem. In waiting on the return line at Home Depot I watched people return one year old telephones, dead plants, even a barbecue packed in a Walmart box. These people had 'balls.' They took it all back. Good customer relations, but could Home Depot afford this? I wouldn't buy the stock. I finally purchased forty-four cabinet pulls for the kitchen.

Roy would put them on. "No big deal." The problem was that on Monday of the third week of July, Roy didn't show up. We figured it was, as he said, "No big deal." We didn't worry about it but when he didn't show up on Tuesday, Stan told us that Roy was a gambler. He had gone off to the Bally's casino on Friday night. Maybe he had struck it rich and didn't need to put our cabinet doors back on!

We telephoned from Sam's gatehouse and got no answer. We got Roy's address and found his home, a modest ranch up Tatum Boulevard in North Phoenix. We didn't like imposing but he had our doors, money and friendship. We were worried. His wife answered the door and said he was sick, was sleeping and would be at our house tomorrow. We knew something was wrong. The smell of beer permeated the inside of the house. We hoped we didn't have a problem, but that night Roy called and confessed to us that he had a hot streak at the card tables and then lost a good deal of money…and had too much to drink. He was remorseful as my wife talked to him for over two hours on the telephone, commiserating, coaxing, supporting. He had been a member of gambler's anonymous for five years and this was the first time he had gone off the wagon. He swore to us he had stopped now.

Roy showed up at 6 A.M. on Wednesday, early even for him, and begged us not to tell what had happened. It would jeopardize his reputation at the Casbah. We fed him coffee and cigarettes for the rest of the day, keeping him going. He looked peaked, but hung the chandelier and went home to put the third coat of enamel on the doors. He was our friend for life, a good man who had strayed My wife had become an analyst as well as a home designer.

The incident was forgotten by mutual agreement. The next day Roy battled with the Italian kitchen fixtures. The instructions were written in Italian, German and French. No English. The lamp store must have gotten a bargain on European surplus. But being resourceful, Roy figured out the connections and the three lights were hanging from the high, whitewashed ceiling by noon. They looked 'outstanding' as Casey Stengel used to say.

By the end of the week we had the cabinet doors on and the pulls. There were so many of them that Roy ran through two batteries on his electric screwdriver. But we were making progress. Stan had gotten half the kitchen floor done by the end of week three. He also suggested we redo the wet bar and kitchen countertops. Since the floor was so expensive, we figured to leave the old tile on. It blended with the travertine. Stan suggested doing the fireplace too. He gave us a price he swore was more than fair. I kidded him that he must have liked it here. It looked like a secure job through the fall. He just smiled. Roy verified the price and so did Tim Reilly when we returned to purchase granite. Our rational for going ahead was that this was to be our home for a long time and we couldn't cheap out on anything…if you got it, spend it! There ain't no tomorrow. Tim was like an old friend now and we spent another lunch with him before selecting a rose and black stone for the kitchen and more travertine for the fireplace and wet bar. While we were at it the three caballeros, Roy, Stan and Don, recommended that we buy a new kitchen sink and faucet. Why not? So back we went to the Pavilion's Home Depot…a circular shopping center of at least 50 stores and ten restaurants and a multiplex theater…with one way in and out off Pima Road…Smart engineering! I like sitting for twenty minutes waiting for the traffic light to change. I bought a kitchen sink and faucet. What the hell. We were living high buying everything…including the proverbial kitchen sink. At least we wouldn't need new toilets…I hoped!

14

More shopping

On our many shopping expeditions our two most paramount needs were a dining room set and a new mattress. We scoured the big chains and found nothing suitable. We needed a 54 inch round table and six chairs. We considered wood, glass tops, metal…but as the days went by, we hadn't yet found it. My wife continued to say she'd know it when she saw it, but I was beginning to believe that it didn't exist to be seen.

We visited Karl the bed maker and were pleased with the head board. Another week and we would have the 'ocean wave.' We talked about our problems with the dining room and Karl came through for us. He could make a table base of iron, match it to the chandelier and design six chairs . He sketched for ten minutes and we agreed on a one chair trial for $150. the chair should be thirty-eight inches high. No problem. Next week we would have the test chair. If we approved, we could have the other five within a month. He called a friend of his and order a bevel edged glass top, three-eighths of an inch thick. Now we had 'gonnections.'

When we called a week later Karl told us the chair was ready but seemed awfully tall. We drove to the shop in Mesa and were bowled over to discover a terrific artful designer chair, but Karl had mistakenly thought the thirty-eight inches was from seat to back top, not floor to top. Wow! We had a giant's throne. Without panic he assured us he could remedy the problem by cutting twelve inches off the back. We liked the design and told him to proceed. We would get material for the seat cushions later. Oh yes. The backs were solid one and one-quarter inch steel and weighed a ton. Nobody would steal these babies! Just eating at our house might give one a hernia. Oh yeah. Mine had not yet 'popped' out. Shortly it would.

Mattresses proved to be my next Waterloo. We checked the department stores and found their prices way too high. We visited furniture stores. I was getting to know Robb and Stuckey, Breuners and Mehegians better than my own house which was still under siege by 'the boys.' Maybe I could work a deal to live in one of their showrooms for a while? Their bedding was also way overpriced. We hit the mattress outlets. Now they all carry the same brands: Sealy, Serta, Simmons, Sterns and Foster. But the models have different names for each sales outlet so we couldn't comparison shop by calling Dial a Mattres(leave out the 's'). There were choices to make: pillow tops, firm, extra firm, soft, wool tops...everything but beds of nails. We found that the less you talked, the faster the salesman came down in price.

"How much for this one?"

"$999."

"Hm. A bit high."

"Today, we have a weekend special. $899." It was Wednesday!

"Hmm." A moment to mull.

"Well, since you're a new resident...$799. And delivery in 24 hours."

"Hmm." Did we need it this fast? The bed was still a week away.

"Try it. Lay on it. Roll over." I did, feeling like a dog being put through his paces. "Arf, Arf! " I bounced around on three. To tell you the truth, they all felt good.

"This has 660 coils. This 440. But the gauge of the springs is important. And the construction of the frame. Guaranteed for ten years. This one for twenty." The facts came flying at us. Who cared? I just wanted to sleep, not live on the damned thing! These guys were mattress mavens.

"Hmm."

"Look. I'll throw in a Harvard frame and mattress cover on this queen. $700. Bottom line."

Boy, could I bargain. "Sold." I signed the papers. I now owned a second mattress and spring. I could have guests. I mean other than Stan, Don and Roy.

Back at the ranch, Stan had finished the kitchen floor running the vinyl hose from the R.O. to the refrigerator under the travertine. God forbid it ever sprang a leak. As far as I was concerned this floor was down for eternity.

The ice machine was on the fritz and we called on the appliance warranty contract. It cost us $35 for the call to learn that the wire lever was out of its proper place. Genius that I am, I never thought to look! Another humiliation. I had been beaten by the dishwasher and the refrigerator. Was the microwave next?

We received our first electric bill from the power company. It was for an astounding $375…for one month. How could I turn the air conditioner down? The guys had to work. Maybe I should have listened to P.J.….J.P. but this we would have to live with for now. The guys were busting their chops and had to stay cool.

Roy had installed the kitchen cabinet doors. Of course we forgot that new hinges were necessary to match the pulls. Back to Home Depot at the Pavilions. They're all out. We call the store on Bell Road. Success! Another fifteen miles, more gas and time. My car is programmed to find the Home Depot triumvirate by automatic pilot. Why go to one when you can visit all three? If Home depot had a frequent flyer plan I would be a leading candidate. You know…visit once a day for ten consecutive days and you get a free package of light bulbs. Twenty days and you can have a toilet seat, vinyl or wood…and so on.

Roy puts them on. The kitchen is done…well sort of. There are still the counter tops, sink, faucet and removal of dust and dirt. Hell, you can't have everything! It's now July 25th. It's been a hell of a '2 weeks.'

15

Nearly finished. Free at last!

Stan put in the final touches on the floor on August 13th and did a masterful job with the granite on the kitchen countertops. He was as proud of the job as we were and took several photographs for future clients. We gladly agreed to show the job any time he wished. As it turned out, Clifford and Frederic hired Stan to do some tile work on a rental unit they owned, so we would still be seeing the boys, although we wouldn't have to feed their sugar habit. The job would take two weeks so I knew we would have them around through October! We had our final chocolate chip cookie breakfast and toasted the job with the last cans of Pepsi Cola that morning. Interestingly, Stan did not do the travertine sealing himself, instead contracting the job out to a tall, lanky, bearded fellow, Lee, who turned out to be a pediatric resident at Phoenix Children's Hospital. Lee did the work part time and turned out to be as good a craftsman as Stan. The only problem was he kept canceling appointments because of hospital emergencies. When I told him my son was also a resident in California, he warmed right up to us. He finally showed up to do the job which took all day. The odor of the sealant was a killer and he asked us if we had scorpions, which were driven out of their holes by the chemical. I don't blame the little critters; it drove us out too. We told him we didn't but that night, like Macbeth, my 'mind was full of scorpions.' Because of our common bond, Lee cleaned up the atrium and car port of all the white stains for no extra charge. He used muriatic acid and I thought he'd burn the bricks away but when the smoke and fumes cleared, the white was gone and the floor intact. I just wouldn't be able to walk barefoot outside for a while!. When he left, the place actually looked shiny new and along with all the stone work, fresh paint, new sink and door handles, the house was shaping up into what we had hoped for. Miraculously the carpet was installed in a day, with two minor complications. First, the installers had to use quick set to build up a slight incline where the travertine left off at the entry to the master bedroom. The men wanted to charge us an extra $100 for the job, but I took exception to this and called the carpet store, using my meanest New York attitude to lambaste the rug lady with their negligence in not allowing for the stone build up, the cheapness of their demand and three other 'barbs.' She gave me no argument and the job was done with no extra fee. Score one more for the good guys!

The second glitch was the installer's needing a staple gun to tack down the carpet on the stairs. Believe it or not, this 'genius of nap' had forgotten his at the warehouse which was on the west side of Phoenix. Wanting the job done today, I drove to get it, learning another area of the city, and returned two hours later. They should have paid me for the time and effort, but there was no way I was going to let these guys leave without finishing. A new problem arose when the wife chastised me for wearing shoes on the new carpet, so now I have to get used to walking around the house barefoot, and I'm not even Japanese!

Karl and his helper delivered the bed the next day and spray painted the frame to get the exact gold tint desired. The bed was a heavy sucker, but fit right in, not diagonally as Mikey White Pants wanted, but perpendicular to the long wall. Mikey did install an ornate grape leaf curtain frame ten feet above the headboard and swept metallic lame bronze , gold and green fabric down from it. Although a feminine touch, the 'Ocean Wave' rolled! I kidded that the bedroom looked like a French whore's boudoir. Mikey didn't take kindly to my joke. It was a good thing Stan wasn't around. Roy installed a hospital television shelf on the opposite wall to keep the floor clear and along with two odd sized night tables we picked up at an antique store the day before when we were exiled by the sealant odor, a leather bench sofa and stool and two Moroccan star lamps, the room was nearly done. The kitchen table went where it belonged. My wife found a large artificial palm at a close out sale and this went into the corner by the window. The room looked as if it belonged in 'Architectural Digest.' I was afraid to go into it for fear of upsetting its order. I guess I wouldn't be able to throw my dirty socks and underwear on the floor anymore!

To finish the job, Karl brought the six 'throne' chairs and dining table base. They were a perfect match to the chandelier, so doing the decorating ass backwards paid off after all. The glass table top arrive two days later and I even 'inherited' a tape measure when one of the workmen left it and told me to keep it when I telephoned him. I guess after all the money we paid, it was a small bonus.

The living room was a problem...why not? It was relatively narrow and Mikey White Pants suggested a sectional sofa to wrap around the corner, approximately ten by eight feet. The trouble was the sectionals in the design center on Thomas Road, the one in the Air Park on North Hayden Road, Robb and Stucky, Mehegians, Breuner's and even Levitz (of all places), had only oversized, overpriced pieces. You notice my familiarity with the neighborhood now? Clifford was amazed that we had found places in South Phoenix which we later learned was the Arizona equivalent of Harlem and Bedford-Stuyvesant. But we were New Yorkers and feared nothing...in the daytime! Mikey White Pants had failed on this one also. I felt badly for him, but not my wallet. Being resourceful, through our growing grapevine of sources, we got a lead on an upholsterer in a Tempe industrial park who could make a sofa from any sketch or photograph. The wife cut out a dozen pictures from home decor magazines. My periodical subscription bills were ever growing to equal my electric bill!

Alan and Laurie, the owners, turned out to have a daughter in pre-med at Northern Arizona University and a son in high school who aspired to being an actor. We talked for an hour about Broadway theater and the tribulations of medical school before we committed to a two piece sectional at a fair price. It would take six weeks to construct and we would be called in to see it in the process. The wife ordered fabric from Mimi's on Delancey Street in New York (ah, the old neighborhood) and we even picked out the pillow filler and tested its firmness a few weeks later.

Our guilt about not buying from Mikey White Pants was somewhat assuaged when we ordered a pair of living room chairs from his store which ended up giving us another headache. As usual a six week order took twelve and ironically we saw the same chairs in 'Z' Gallery, a chain with branches all over the place for $20 less and available with the material we wanted within a month! It was fun calling Mikey every day for six weeks, threatening to do everything to him from stripping off his white pants, to cutting his atrocious neckties…he finally refused to take our calls, instead hiding behind a sweet girl who was a receptionist at the store. We were on a first name basis in no time. Live and learn, God bless Mikey White Pants! We took an eternal vow never to get involved with a decorator (there, I said it!) again.

We had become used to eight hour shopping days and now that our palette, as Mikey called it, was completed and accessories being bought, we felt a kind of post natal depression. We had a conflict between bathroom towel bars or rings which my wife won (rings), and another battle over where to position my stereo (in the loft closet), but other than awaiting a desk and the sectional sofa, we now could turn our attention to finding art objects to warm up the place. After paint, flooring and door pulls, how hard could it be?

16

For art's sake

We had been here for two months now, withstood the heat (one day the temperature actually hit 121 degrees), I know, it's a dry heat, it'll just kill you, and have even come to know where Camelback Mountain interrupts the through streets. We've been perusing classified ads for yard… pardon me, estate sales, although some of these 'estates' look like share cropper shacks to me. Image is everything!

We've been to several art galleries in Old Scottsdale and find cowboy art not to our taste. The weekend shows seem to be filled with 'wannabe' painters. I can't believe some of the stuff shown: cactus in one hundred three sexual positions, the Grand Canyon inside out and upside down, painted plastic cattle skulls with and without horns. A lot of the desert scapes look like children's numbered paintings. These 'darlings of the paint brush' (I won't honor them with the title 'artist…' oddist' might be more suitable) dress up like Wild Bill Hickock, Buffalo Bill Cody and Annie Oakley, complete with Stetson ten gallon hats, spurs, knee high boots, chaps and fringe all over including their jock straps. They look like refugees from a 1950's television western. I wonder if any of these Hoot Gibson's have ever been on a horse. But their stuff sells. One vendor actually will come to your home to match his paint colors to your furniture. Art on order…have brush will travel…Picasso would not approve!

Michael Boloker

We found an excellent source for prints and original pieces in the Scottsdale Air Park, an industrial area filled with small companies of every sort. They had exclusive rights to several artists and we took home a half dozen paintings on a trial basis and made several swaps over the next week. I made daily round trips and wished I could have a frequent flyer program for this place as well as Home Depot. The framing was unique and beautiful and often more expensive than the art itself. The artist, as usual, makes less than his agent and the gallery. It's the eternal conflict between art and commerce with commerce winning every time.

We blundered into an art swindle naively phoning a classified ad we had pursued in the Arizona Republic for an estate sale: "house featured in Architectural Digest, furniture, paintings, art objects." It turned out to be in northwest Phoenix, next to a shopping mall and from the exterior, looked far from what the ad promised, but it had taken us over an hour to arrive so we went in. A heavy, middle aged fellow named Robert Gaccione greeted us at the door, dressed in what had to be an Armani suit, Gucci shoes, heavy horn rimmed spectacles and a cultured, articulate speaking voice that sounded like Frasier Crane from television. The place was decorated to the nines. There were oriental rugs, paintings, tapestries, beautiful lamps and large expensive furniture. You never know what you'll find behind closed doors. We liked a pair of matching pen and ink sketches of musicians done in the abstract, and a large multi-media collage framed dramatically with black matte and thick gold plate. They were striking pieces. We also liked a beige print Nepalese carpet, 6 x 9 foot, which would go perfectly in our living room. Gaccione wanted $1,000 for the pair of sketches and $750 for the mixed media . The carpet was a Tafenkian, priced at $6,000. We had seen these at ABC Carpet in New York for more money. The story we got was that his brother owned the house, preferring to live in a less affluent area, furnished it expensively with the best his San Francisco designer could find, but had to move to Australia for business purposes. Robert was extremely personable and impressed on us that he wanted to sell the contents of the house expeditiously and the prices were half their original value. He could produce information on the artists to verify their originality and value. Before we laid out that much money we needed time to think and told him we would call within two days. He impressed on us not to tarry. He had prospective buyers coming all day.

Of course I was skeptical. Were the paintings really worth that much? "The framing alone is," the wife claims. "It goes perfectly with the floor and sofa," she continues.

"We'll sleep on it." I picture dollars floating out of what remained of my retirement bonus account. And I wasn't sure of the abstract paintings. I had read recently that a craftsman is an artist with skill and no imagination. He makes baskets and pots. An artist with imagination and no skill is an abstractionist. Clever. Did I want abstract work in my living room?

Mr. Gaccione helped make up our minds. He telephoned the next day with an offer we couldn't refuse. The three paintings for $1250 and the carpet for $4,500. "Hmm." I remembered my mattress negotiation. "Well, I know I can get a Tafenkian in New York for $3500."

"All right. Take it for $4,000. And I'll deliver it today. I have to be in your area."

"Fine." So much for thought and consultation. The wife was flying. The deal was made, although he insisted on payment by a local bank check. No problem. I would transfer funds tomorrow and post date the check. True to his word he delivered the goods an hour later. We shook hands on the deal and he even promised to mail me the biographies of the artists, which he did a week later.

We hung the pictures and rolled out the carpet, pleased with our high quality bargains. The kicker to all this occurred two weeks later when Rochelle brought over our art purchases from the Air Park gallery and noticed the pair of sketches and the abstract. She asked where we had purchased them and we proudly told her of our find.

The story then unfolded that made our jaws drop. Mr. Gaccione used to own a gallery which her agents supplied. He closed shop abruptly one night and took off with all the paintings worth well over many thousands of dollars. He declared bankruptcy.

It was learned that he had done this a number of times over the years and had 'possessed' a lot of artwork and furnishings from various Valley establishments. Now he ran these alleged estate sales weekly, cash on delivery, and made a lucrative living. Rochelle knew the paintings we purchased because they were among those she had lost. There was no problem for us, she assured. She described Gaccione accurately, right down to his Guccis.

So we realized we had indeed gotten a good price on the rug and paintings. I felt badly for Rochelle, but there was nothing she could do and we had bought six pieces from her. I just hoped the cops wouldn't come to our house someday and repossess our purchases! I am a worrier. But as of today, the things are still here, proudly displayed. It makes for a good story when company comes. And sure enough, Robert Gaccione's ad is in the Arizona Republic classified section every Sunday, as regular as the comics!

17

Is there a doctor in the house?

I still felt kind of temporary about our place at the Casbah until those Arcadia doors came back to haunt me. I suppose being injured and slinking back to my refuge turned the house into my home. It was a safe haven from the ravages done to my aging body by surgery.

One day in October while toweling off from a shower I noticed a lump protruding from my lower abdomen on the right size. I was either pregnant, growing a third leg, a second penis, or….suffering from a hernia. I checked with my son who at first evaded the issue like most medical specialists (what had I spawned?) by saying he only knew how to deal with premature babies. Did you ever notice how doctors train for a dozen years, study, take exams, work eighty hour weeks, but only know one area of the human body, usually six inches by six inches? I pressed him and he concurred that I probably had an inguinal hernia.

"But it doesn't hurt and when I lie down it goes away." I felt like a child as our roles were reversed. Maybe if I put iodine on it it would go away. "No, Dad…you have the classic signs. Get into a doctor and take care of it before it gets worse. And don't strain yourself."

Right. How could I avoid moving furniture to satisfy the wife's daily whims to redecorate with our new purchases? I read up on my 'problem' in the medical books and learned about this new "protrusion" on my body. Actually it was the first thing I'd grown other than fat in thirty years. Since my youth I had lost hair, teeth, strength and my perfect eye sight, so maybe this was a renaissance.

Now I was forced to find a surgeon, not an easy task for someone raised in New York City, the Mecca for highly priced, qualified Jewish doctors. My mother would turn over in her grave if I dared not use a Lansman! Did they have this species in Arizona?

My medical insurance gave me the option of using my own physician and paying twenty percent of the fees or selecting one of their partici- pating doctors at a nominal co-payment of $8 per visit. The hospital costs were covered. In checking my health insurance roster, I felt as if I were reading the Bombay, India telephone directory. Were there any American born and trained doctors in the plan? I found only two sur- geons in Arizona, one in Tucson who specialized in hand surgery. If I went to him could I claim I was growing a new hand in my abdomen to get the food directly into my stomach faster? A medical miracle? No chance. The other was a general surgeon in Phoenix with the name of Wilbur Smith. Can't be more American than that. I telephoned his office and begged and pleaded for an appointment. I needed a referral from my regular physician and being a new patient had to wait a month for an opening. "What if I were near death's door?"

"Then we'd take you," answered the nurse. "Actually Doctor Smith is just recovering from heart bypass surgery so he has cut back on his schedule."

This was not good news. What if he keeled over the operating table with my guts cut open? I figured I'd better go ahead anyway. "Well, I'm crawling up the stairs to the door with a bulging hernia about to stran- gulate(I had read up on this)."

"Come in tomorrow at 7:30 A.M."

Doesn't this guy sleep? I called my internist in New York who said he would check for me. He might have a connection in Phoenix. A friend of his from med school had settled down there ten years ago. He would get back to me.

The next morning I was greeted by a young receptionist who asked for my insurance card before saying good morning and handed me a clipboard with a three page medical history form to fill out. I had forgotten my reading glasses and struggled in the semi-dark waiting room for fifteen minutes giving such relevant data as my sister's age, the size of my big toe and who would pay the bills if I were to croak. I didn't even have a chance to skim the stack of 1986 'Time' magazines. Doctor Smith must either like night club atmosphere or be saving on his electric bills judging by the dearth of illumination in the office. I did not have good vibes here.

Half expecting to find an Arizona version of young doctor Frankenstein, Dr. Wilbur Smith turned out to be a tall, bald, bearded old gentleman, looking more like a cowboy than Jack Palance in the movie "City Slickers." His face was leathery creased, eyes clear as ice blue crystal, cold and piercing. He wore a white lab coat over a western plaid shirt complete with string tie, black jeans and cowboy boots. There was a diploma on the wall from the University of Arizona medical school but my eyes could not read the date. I hoped he was a genuine surgeon and not a veterinarian. He was elderly and intimidating. I dared not cross him for fear he had a six shooter hidden in a shoulder holster.

He looked over my medical history ordered me to drop my pants and probed the area of my malady. "Yup. Hernia. Got to be fixed. What do you say?"

No small talk with this cowboy. "Well what do you suggest?"

"Ain't no doubt about it. Cut it open, sew it up and rest it. Should be good as new in a few months. I can do the job next month."

"Shouldn't it be right away?"

"Could be. No more harm can happen if you don't lift. Take it easy. But I'm only working a limited schedule right now until I'm healed myself. So I can't do it right away. You'll have to wait."

"What procedure will you use?" I got no answer. "I read about laproscopy? You know, three small incisions and minor cutting?"

"Don't like it. Don't really trust them new methods. Heard they have more of a chance of coming back. Your rupture I mean. Old method is best. Cut and sew it up. 95% it'll hold. Unless you start weight lifting too soon." He laughed heartily. "And you Easterners don't appear to be real heavy workers." He guffawed again. "You could always wear a support. A truss." Right! It wasn't going to happen.

I felt intimidated, patronized. It was uncomfortable and something I hadn't felt since I was a high schooler browbeaten by my old math teacher, old lady Slattery, when I didn't know my parts of speech.

"I'd rather not wait. I read about strangulated hernias and want this taken care of."

"Well, the best I can do for you is in six weeks. Of course I can send you to someone else. Young doctor named Bruce. Jay Bruce. He might be available."

I wanted nothing to do with Dr. Smith. I didn't hesitate. "Good. Call him." I was sweating anxiously, me a grown man of 57. I was afraid he would refuse.

"I'll have my girl do it." He left the room abruptly and I did too. The receptionist gave me Dr. Jay Bruce's telephone number. He was in surgery right now and his office didn't open until 11. I was done with Dr. Wilbur Smith forever.

I drove home and stopped with Sam the gate guard to pick up my mail, telling him about Dr. Smith and my hernia just to talk to somebody. "You ought to try Dr. Bruce. Mr. Bader in unit 101 had an operation with him last year. He's supposed to be the best."

My God! Sam knew everything about his place, even the doctors. He was becoming indispensable to my Arizona survival. When I got home there was a message on my answering machine from my New York doctor. Amazingly his old friend was one Dr. Jay Bruce also. It had to be fate.

I was in Bruce's office the next morning, filled out another three page form, this time in good light with my reading glasses on, had my insurance card copied, and met a short, curly-haired bespectacled studious looking man who was personable. He was from the new school of physicians who drew pictures to explain everything. His art work was worse than a kindergarteners, with large birds and an oval shaped sun over a sketch of my body, but what he said jibed with what I had read and he convinced me that the best way to go was the tried and true method of cutting and repairing the tear in the intestinal wall with a synthetic patch. He sounded like a plumber in discussing my most precious body. It was a simple surgery, done in an outpatient clinic next to Scottsdale Memorial Hospital, and could be done on Friday morning. He would use a local anesthetic. I could be home in three hours. I agreed, signed the forms and made a date, so to speak.

I was not nervous at all about the procedure and showed up bright and confident at 7 A.M. to fill out another bundle of forms, have the procedure explained to me as if I were a moron, and was wheeled into the back room to disrobe and be shaved, and I don't mean my face. I suppose by the time a human gets to be my age there is nothing that can be done that humiliates me anymore. I have been washed, shaved, cut, caressed, poked, prodded and fondled by all manner of creatures in my journey through life, so this was really nothing new. I was cool, pondering the state of my 56 year old body which now would have another artificial part. I had a synthetic buckle around my left eyeball from a detached retina, skin on the bridge of my nose taken from behind my ear to patch up the removal of a basal cell skin cancer, several screws in an ankle bone, not to mention contact lenses, dental bridges and other body alterations. If I had lived in an earlier century I wouldn't have survived past forty. Science!

Dr. Bruce was supposed to be in at 8:30 for the procedure, pardon me, but he called in to say that he would be a little late. Finishing up an emergency at Scottsdale Memorial North. Hmmm. Had his scalpel slipped on someone this morning? I hoped he was as good as Sam the gate guard said. I was having second thoughts when he came bustling into the pre-op room wearing his green scrubs and a cap, his shoes covered with booties. It was hard to recognize him, but he was all business. He ordered the anesthetist to go ahead with the sedative to relax me and as I was being wheeled into the operating room, watching the ceiling tiles and lights flash above me, what could I do but go with the flow. I figured I would listen to everything being done and try to act nonchalant as they cut me open but I was sabotaged as the doctor asked me to start counting backwards and I got to ninety-one when the lights went out.

I woke up to find my wife next to me and a nurse explaining that I should take it easy. The surgery was over. Before I could orient myself, Dr. Bruce wa explaining that everything went well and after I was fully awake and passed water, I could leave. He would see me in one week.

He was gone. The whole thing had taken a little over an hour. I felt fine and was anxious to leave. The nurse showed me my taped over incision, about six inches of adhesive where my little 'lumpkin' had been. Would they let me take the piece home in a jar? No. I wondered what they did with all these sawed off body parts? Did they keep a pack of hungry dogs out back?

When I struggled out of bed fifteen minutes later to 'pass water' I found that the 'passer' took a long time to unload and the stream a mere trickle that took a good five minutes. "It'll take time before the anesthesia wears off. It's normal," the nurse reassured me. I just wanted to get out of the damned place and go home.

Home. This is the first time I really felt like I belonged here. It was a hell of a way to arrive at this moment, but I wasn't arguing.

As it turned out, excuse me for being graphic, I did have trouble urinating for the next two days. It burned, gave little relief and alarmed me. I felt as if I had to go all the time. I called Dr. Bruce on Saturday night to interrupt his theater date, was apologetic, and explained my concern. He again told me a man my age often has prostate problems.

I had never had them and objected to his instant diagnosis.

"Well, you can go down to the emergency room to get catheterized and that should take the pressure off your bladder. Otherwise wait a week. Give the old plumbing a chance." Boy, he was hardly sympathetic toward my malady. So much for bedside manner.

No way in the world I would have that done to me. I thought of Dr. Wilbur Smith and wondered if he had done the surgery would I have had this complication. I laughed. Probably be dead now. I would bear the discomfort and hoped the old body would come around. It did.

I was walking in two days, had no pain whatsoever except a bit of soreness when I got out of bed, and was anxious to start doing some exercises. Upon my visit to Dr. Bruce the following week, I saw the scar for the first time, pink and nasty, and he assured me it would be gone in a few months. "No running or straining for a month."

"What about swimming?"

"No."

"Would I spring a leak?"

This brought a smile to his hairy cheeks. "When you begin physical exercising again, don't push too hard. Come back in a month."

So it all went well. Of course I got the bill promptly the first of the month and had to wrestle with my insurance company for proper payments. I also received an unexpected bill from the anesthesiologist who I saw for about ten seconds. $400 for him. Not a bad way to make a living.

My first long walk was at the Fountain Hills Arts and Crafts show where the wife walked me up and down rows of cowboy art, pottery, leather goods, Indian fry bread and salsa concessions. I had samples to eat, which burned my mouth out, and in a way blessed my hernia because it gave me an excuse to skip half the damned show on the pretense of fatigue and discomfort.

So I won't be lifting any more Arcadia doors. I hope Dr. Wilbur Smith retires. I empathize with my friend Henry who has prostate problems and has to urinate every two hours of his life with minimal relief. I don't know how he does it. I had only one week of this excruciating burning and discomfort and I was ready to surrender.

As an addendum to this Arizona medical adventure I wish to inform you of two further incidents. First, the wife searched out a gynecologist, followed the recommendation of a neighbor. Sam the gate guard couldn't help us with this one. The doctor turned out to be all right but the series of lab tests she recommended had to be taken at the Mayo Clinic. This is supposed to be one of the finest facilities in the world, but it's such a huge place that you get treated as if you didn't exist. She sat in a large assembly hall with a numbered slip in her hands as the electric board in front flashed the integers. You felt like one of the herd. They didn't use names and the wait was long. Now I know what cows feel like waiting in the slaughterhouse for the call!

And the prices they charge are double what another lab would. It took me six months to clear the fees with my insurance company and the doctor buffers herself with middle management clerks and case numbers rather than addressing any problems herself. In telephoning the clinic to get the matter straightened out, I must have been put on hold for a total of ten hours until I could finally get any cooperation from the billing department. They're worse than the department of motor vehicles. Is there anything worse than telephoning an office and hearing, "Will you hold please?" Click. Well thanks for giving me the courtesy of answering. And then the inevitable tape comes on with, "Your call is important to us. Please be patient until one of our operators is available." Over and over for twenty minutes. It's easy to give up. I once threatened an airline operator by telling her if I could reach my hand through the line, I would strangle her. She informed me that she didn't have to take this abuse and hung up. So much for diplomacy! The problem now is that we have to find dentists! I shudder at the thought. Sam the gate guard better have someone for us or I'm going to become suicidal! Sometimes I think we'd be better off letting our teeth rot out and our bodies go. To hell with longevity. It's the quality of life that counts and battling the medical hierarchy ain't worth it.

18

Arizona honeymoon: period of adjustment

Settling into my new Arizona lifestyle came gradually in a series of initiation experiences. They were surprising, enlightening, puzzling and somewhat disorienting for someone who had lived in New York for most of his adult life. Now that I had the time, I started to poke around and adjust to the area, its natives and customs. It wasn't easy.

I realized I was in foreign territory when I went to the Scottsdale Public Library and the sign next to the front entrance read, "Deadly weapons not allowed in building." The only deadly weapon I ever carried in New York was a ball point pen. I am also the kind of automobile driver who takes offense when driver's cut me off, fail to signal on a turn or tailgate. I curse, point fingers and vent my rage to the offender whenever possible. I always thought New York City cabbies were the worst drivers in the world, but since moving to Phoenix, I've changed my mind. In New York we called dare devil drivers 'cowboys.' Here the drivers are literally cowboys! Arizona drivers are as cut throat on the road as they are polite off it. I told my neighbor about my complaints and he cautioned me not to demonstrate my irritation overtly or one of these offenders is liable to pull out a weapon and blast me away. Another reminder that I now live in the wild West. While waiting at a red light on

Scottsdale Road the other day, the driver in the next car was playing with a rifle. Shades of "Easy Rider."

I've learned to slow down here. I enjoy the courtesy displayed in stores by clerks who personally show me where items are. I take pleasure when asked in the supermarket if I've found everything all right. If one says 'no,' the checker will leave her register and escort you to the item leaving the customers on line to stew. Not smart policy! It's comical to me that everyone pays grocery bills at the register by personal check. I was standing on line behind a woman the other day who pulled out a desk top checkbook and proceeded to spend fifteen minutes paying a bill for $3.41. She even took time to calculate her balance, then left the market and got into a Mercedes. I cannot get out of a store without having a thirty-minute conversation with a sales clerk. They always ask me if I'm from New York, my accent is a dead give away, and then proceed to tell me of their visit to the Big Apple. I courteously reciprocate and ask where they are originally from and tell them my adventures in their hometown. I've made many new friends this way.

In the summer months the main topic of conversation is the weather. The heat seems to be not only a preoccupation with residents but with television stations as well. When it rained one day in July, I never heard so many stories about the experiences of locals in my life. It was a classic case of media overkill. There was a feature on a traffic pile up on Route 17 caused by slick roads, a roof blown off a school in Glendale, a dust storm in North Phoenix. Haven't people here ever experienced rain before? Everyone seemed to have his own individual raindrop. It was like the second coming of the great flood!

I was so thankful when Charles Barkley was traded away from the Suns that I made a sacrifice to my newly bought Kachina doll. Sir Charles, as he's reverently called here, seemed to be more important than even the weather around these parts. Now in New York we have the Yankees, the Knicks, the Rangers, the Giants, the Jets and even the Islanders, but we keep sports in perspective. Muggings, rapes and murders, those old standbys, take priority in the media, not to mention politics. Well, Barkley did say he was going to run for governor of Alabama after he retired from the N.B.A.

The television stations illustrate the homogenization of America. Each network has a newscast at exactly the same time with co-anchors, usually a white male mannequin and a Black, Mexican or Asian American female . The half hour of each telecast is compartmentalized in precise bites, each identical to the other, even down to commercials: local crime news, a human interest story, a brief C.N.N. overview of national and international news, the weather and sports. They even flash the score of the Suns game every five minutes. Really important stuff! The weather man is either an elderly pseudoscientific meteorologist or a cute, Miss America contestant type. The sportscaster is often a younger, frustrated jock who banters in adolescent prattle with the anchors. Turn on channels 3, 5, 10, 12 or 15 and you get equal doses of the same 'cold soup' at exactly the same time. Thank God for channel 8, if you can tolerate the seemingly endless campaigns for financing from to support the public station.

I felt totally out of place when I went out to dinner with some new acquaintances and was the only man in the restaurant wearing a sport jacket and dark pants. I even wore socks! I'll have to get used to dressing down, although I find this a pleasant experience after a lifetime of ties and jackets. My wife hasn't worn a pair of high heels since July. She's panting to go somewhere so that she can wear a long skirt. I think I'll have to take her to San Diego.

I've talked about furniture stores earlier. Now that we're looking for accessories to add 'tone' to our dream house, it's become more futile. In all the big chain stores there is little offered that's not built to gigantic scale to fill the many 3,000 square foot homes being built in the Valley. The other notable quality is the preponderance of neutral colors. Everything is off white or beige. What happened to red, blue and purple? Oh yes. That's in the many Phoenix Suns tee shirts I see kids wearing everywhere. Even the Mexican furniture shops charge four times the prices of items you can buy in Nogales.

I've been trying to get my backyard landscaped for the past three weeks. I've got the man. Roy recommended him with Steve the gate guard's blessing.

We've agreed on a price, but he's always working in Fountain Hills and until he gets finished, he can't come to do my yard. I have biweekly conversations with Jesus and he's a lovely man who promises he will be at my place by next Tuesday. Those Tuesdays have been October 1, 8th, 15th and 22nd. Maybe tomorrow! Manana is something I'm learning to deal with as a new Phoenician.

As far as time here goes, maybe the fact that Arizona does not go on Daylight Savings Time with with the rest of the nation should have clued me in. I moved to the Valley determined to slow down my New York life style and relax as a nearly retired Arizonan should. No more high blood pressure, impatience on bank lines, pushing and shoving to get ahead of the next guy. I would be calm, easy going and courteous. I should have known better. I have failed miserably in this endeavor. I still get annoyed at the myriad frustrations I've had with what my wife and I call living on 'Arizona Time.'

For instance take the local bagel shop. Now in New York City it's ritual to have a bagel and coffee on your way to work or on your hour lunch break. You can go into Tal Bagel on First Avenue and get on line behind ten others and still be served within three minutes. There are half a dozen men working at high speed to expedite the orders. It's amazing to watch six grown men dodging and weaving in a space three feet wide by six feet long cutting, toasting, and smearing bagels. And not a cup of coffee spilled! On Sunday morning the lines are twice as long and the orders much more elaborate: dozens of bagels, pounds of lox and sturgeon, vats of cream cheese. But if you wait more than five minutes it's an aberration.

Now in Scottsdale we have a unique system that works (or fails to) on
'Arizona Time.' You stand in line, at first patiently, behind two other
customers for ten minutes until your order is taken by either a teen ager
or an elderly lady (only the bored or desperate work for minimum
wage). Of course they're usually out of the flavored bagel you want.
Sesame is the most popular and God forbid the establishment plans
ahead to have more at peak times. You settle for another flavor. The
clerk inserts the bagel in the cutting machine, a modern day guillotine,
and then into the toaster which can only handle one bagel per minute.
Again, why have a toaster that can handle multiple orders? Then, when
ready, the girl puts on your cream cheese spending time admiring her
sculpting masterpiece. Of course she wears a plastic glove which is
allegedly sanitary, despite her scratching her hair and nose. Is this supposed to be a sterile field? When ready she inserts the bagel into a bag.
The process has taken seven minutes (I timed it). You then take your
goods to the register. There is one cashier and a half dozen people are
ahead of you. This mathematical whiz kid takes drink requests, answers
the telephone and packs the orders. Of course these have priority over
the living customers on line. The man ahead of you slows up in this
snail like approach to completion by having a conversation on his cellu-
lar phone. These are big in Arizona along with pagers. It's a high tech
state. For people who live a slow and leisurely life there sure are a lot of
critical phone conversations that can't wait until you get home or to the
office. At last you get to the register twenty minutes after entering the
shop. The girl asks what you have (honor system), accepts discount
coupons and punches in the total. Your toasted bagel is now cold and
when you mention this, the girl looks at you as if you're crazy. You let it
slide and are finally given a cup for coffee and when you go to the dis-
penser, they are out of decaf! You return, wait three minutes to be
acknowledged, and tell the cashier, who abandons her register and the
backlog of customers to go back into the kitchen to order a new
tankard. You are told the coffee will be out in a minute. You wait, and

wait, and wait. Ho hum! Finally you surrender and take a cup of regular coffee which wires you for the rest of the day. It's 'Arizona Time.' And all I wanted was a quick bagel fix!

Now I learned about store lines my first week here…and I enjoy a conversation with the store clerk. In New York you get an insincere "Have a nice day" and you're out the door. Here you have to have a meaningful relationship with the clerk. I can't be at my Arizona best at 7 A.M. I'm still New York surly. And why do people write checks and use debit cards on the express line? Hey Arizona, learn what the work 'express' means!

Another example of 'Arizona Time' occurs while driving a car waiting to make a left turn at a traffic light. Now first you have to determine if you're in Scottsdale (left after green), or Phoenix (left before green). By the time you realize what city you're in you've missed the light which is timed to let two cars turn. For some reason they expect you to turn in ten seconds even though there are twelve cars ahead of you. So 'Arizona Time' says stay on line for five light changes and enjoy the scenery for the eighteen minute wait. You can go straight and make a U turn faster! Of course I think the Arizona driving instructors and manual have not taught drivers to proceed into an intersection to turn left. The drivers wait at the corner even on a green light with no one coming in the opposite direction. As the light turns yellow they finally catch on and surge through the turn, nearly colliding with the traffic coming through on green from the left and right. Ah, 'Arizona Time!'

Yesterday I went to get the oil changed in my car at a quick lube station. In New York it takes ten minutes guaranteed or you get your oil service at no charge. Great. I figure in Arizona fifteen minutes…it's hot, they're slow.

I pull in. "No problem. We'll get you right in. Drive up to the second bay." I do. They have me fill out the papers while my car is put on the lift tracks, the hood opened, ready to be serviced. What I didn't realize is that this is 'Arizona Time.' We'll get you in right away, but not out! I sit in the waiting room reading 1995 magazines and trying to watch an old black and white television through a mass of snowy interference. The coffee wagon comes by giving the laborers a fifteen minute break. I am called into the work area at last. Do I want a new air filter, transmission fluid coolant? No. I just had them changed last month. Finally, a half hour later I am done. Or so I thought. The genius clerk punches in my credit card and the receipt charges me $2121.80 instead of $21.80. Oops, a two thousand dollar oil change! He's apologetic for his over-sight and sincere, but it's a good thing I checked the bill. Hurray! It's 'Arizona Time.'

So even though I realize it's hot here in the Valley and I enjoy the cordiality and good manners of the residents, and I have more time because I'm basically retired, I still have a low tolerance for wasted time and inept service. Am I too 'Eastern'? Is it my New York genes? Or is it 'Arizona Time'?

One always hears of New York City being the melting pot of the nation but the more I travel the more I realize that the entire country is becoming a mixed bag of both international and national flavors. Scottsdale is a perfect example of this phenomenon and to focus on this aspect of Valley life I have to look no further than the Casbah. In the house to my left reside Canadians from Toronto, the Yorks. Along the block are people who have migrated here from Connecticut, Vermont, Philadelphia, Kansas, Seattle and Illinois among other American locales. Their religions vary from Jewish to Catholic, Protestant, Mormon, Muslim. Then there are people who winter here from Europe and an unusual couple married over twenty years with the husband, Joe originally from Alabama and the wife, Mary from England. When I greet them I get unusual idioms such as, "Cheerio, you all."

The Chicagoans run around in shorts and tee shirts despite the tem-perature being in the thirty-degree range lately. I shiver in my thickest jacket. I threw away my ice scraper when I moved down here and I'm certainly not enough of a plant lover to wrap my plants to protect them from the night chill. They'll have to fend for themselves. I have enough trouble wrapping myself in quilts to keep warm. I did not move to Arizona for this! The Illini laugh at me.

It took some time to overcome the language barriers with my Toronto friends. I know Canadians are supposed to share a common language with us but I've found that not to be entirely true. They told us about ordering a 'Chesterfield' which I didn't think twice about with this cold weather streak. After all, I could have used this type of coat myself. When they said it was going to cost over $5,000 I was taken aback. Then I found out that a 'Chesterfield' in Canada is a sofa. Of course they laughed at my pronunciation which sounded like 'sofer' to them.

A week later we wanted to play tennis but Bob had to go to buy runners. For what did he need parts to a sled, I thought, until we drove up to a sporting goods store and he bought a pair of sneakers (running shoes in the modern vernacular). His favorite expression is "Oh, yes," which I learned is Canadian for "you know." My schedule is his 'shedyule.'

The Yorks had a visitor from Saskatchewan who told me he lived in a bungalow. I felt sorry for the guy because to live in a small cottage or shack usually indicates poverty. The man then showed me a picture of a rambling ranch house twice the size of mine. Another lesson learned about the differences in Canadian and American English.

The Europeans are all golf crazy. Our friend Joe plays at least three times a week, which costs him a tidy sum I am sure. His goal is to play every golf course in the Phoenix area. He says there are 147 courses and he's up to 91. I kidded him about how fast new golf courses were being built and that he would have a hard time keeping up. And I thought New Yorkers were compulsive!

The Canadians love the outdoors and we've joined a Sunday hiking group. The highlight is brunch afterward at the nearest golf club. We've taken five mile treks in the Superstitions, White Tanks, South Mountain, McDowell, Squaw Peak and the lake region. Usually there are at least a dozen Canadians and us 'New Yawkers.' It looks like the

Edmonton Oilers pursuing two middle aged New York Ranger fans down a desert slope. In the restaurant we are always seated with our backs to the windows so the Canadians can watch the action on the green while scoffing down their eggs. It makes for difficult conversation not to have eye contact with the person you're addressing. But we're getting used to it. I'd rather eat than putt. My wife is most comfortable in high heels. She can walk fifty city blocks in these, but here in the desert I don't think they'd survive, so we broke down and bought hiking shoes and walking sticks. This foot gear is the ugliest conceivable apparel, designed by color blind Asians who do this to get back at us for their slave wages. Purples, greens, orange and turquoise—not exactly Ferragamo's. And to pay twenty dollars for a five-foot stick is just too much! A tree branch for God's sake! Did Moses pay this for his staff? So with language differences, variations in clothes styles and other perspectives, the great melting pot of Scottsdale flourishes with a sense of common pursuits...and humor. In this period of adjustment we'll see which of my two lives will survive. Will it be my New York past or my Arizona present. Jekyll or Hyde...or vice versa?

19

Sexism, sports, food and travel

In finishing up this long, humorous diatribe the great literary themes, sexism, sports, food and travel must be commented upon. Ernest Hemingway addressed them in his writing, so why shouldn't I?

In order to make new friends and acquaintances my wife joined a welcome wagon group. The first meeting was a seminar for new residents to break the ice, so to speak, a difficult task in these hot climes where everybody hunkers down in his air conditioned house for the summer, only coming out in the night like some nocturnal creature. Fifteen women showed up, most matronly, a number divorced and a few elderly with newly retired husbands. The group's leader discussed the popular book "Men are From Mars, Women from Venus." Later that day my wife related the gist of the discussion to me. Many of the ladies had given ultimatums to their husbands that the men had better keep busy during the day and out of their way. It was better when they worked. It was as if their marriages were predicated on this separatism. The divorced women delighted in this denigration of men. To keep the discussion going the hypothetical situation was proposed in which the girls were asked who would they save if both their husband and child were drowning? Most would have saved their child. My wife, repulsed by this sophomoric discussion, more suited to a college freshman seminar than one for supposedly mature women, replied that she would first save me and then hope that in turn my strength would save our son. This was not a popular answer. I suppose in therapy these types of situations are discussed. My wife does not go to a therapist either. We work our problems out. We talk, like each other and enjoy sharing experiences. We have for over thirty years of marriage.

It seems to me seminars like this are childish, time occupiers for women with no sense of purpose. They need something to do and responding to what is in vogue this decade, proceed to bash men. Why not? Movies like "Thelma and Louise," "Antonia's Line," and the popular "First Wives Club" feed this trend. The theme is also reflected in popular literature. There are "The Women's Room" and "Waiting to Exhale" among others. Television goes right along. Was Spiro Agnew right in his estimation that the media are controlled by effete snobs and gays? Feed the sharks what they want. New York Magazine and the Sunday New York Times have featured articles on gays coming out of the closet being so blase now that people don't pay attention to it any more. And then there's "Ellen," everybody's favorite lesbian.

I realize it's politically correct to accept single mothers, lesbians and homosexuals, but can't somebody out there make a case for men? Has the pendulum swung completely the other way so that men are not the pariahs? Do I have to make excuses for liking sports? May I drink a beer instead of white wine? In a restaurant may I order a steak without feeling guilty for not eating roughage? Can I compliment a good looking woman without being accused of sexual abuse? Come on ladies, give a guy a break!

For the first time in my forty years as a New York Giants' football fan I went to see my team play in an arena other than Yankee Stadium in the Bronx or Giants Stadium in the New Jersey Meadowlands because this is the only chance to see my beloved 'Big Blue.' So off I went to Arizona State University Sun Devil's Stadium, recently renamed for the venerable Frank Kush, ex-football coach. Believe me, it ain't the Meadowlands!

It was enlightening and enjoyable even though the hometown Cardinals won the game 31-23. We miss Phil Simms and Lawrence Taylor a lot!

I bought a ticket at Dillards, choosing the cheapest end zone seat at $20 plus a dollar fifty service charge if you please, figuring I could finagle a good seat by giving the usher a few bucks once I was inside. In New Jersey you have to be born to a season ticket holder to get into any game and I used to go once a year with my oldest friend who accepted the $30 as a favor. I had heard on the radio in the morning that there would be 37,000 seats available. That would be unheard of in New York. Parking in the Meadowlands costs ten dollars and you have no choice. It's park here or hit the road, Jack. The stadium is built off the New Jersey Turnpike and there is simply no other place to leave your automobile.

I left my house at noon figuring I would park in a shopping center off Mill Avenue and avoid paying for parking. It took me fifteen minutes to get to Tempe. In New York it would have been a two hour struggle in bumper to bumper traffic. I did this and walked the five short blocks to the stadium to which I arrived at 12:20. On the way I was accosted by scalpers who had $50 seats which they offered for $30 and one proposed to buy my end zone seat for $5. I tried to trade it to him with $5 for one of his but he refused. I'm glad he did. I passed several lots on the way which charged money to park so I was already ahead of the game.

It was a beautiful, sunny seventy degrees, but I had brought a jacket in case it got cold. You haven't felt cold until you sit in Giants Stadium on a forty-degree day, especially in the late afternoon. It was a waste of effort as I sat in the sun for half the game and didn't need even a sweatshirt. Sun- glasses and a tee shirt were sufficient. I had coated my face in sunscreen, a daily routine now that I live in the valley of the sun. This was not NFL football as I had come to know and love it. The gates didn't open until 12:30 so I leisurely ate my sandwich and watched the orderly crowd milling around, many of them wearing Giant blue shirts and hats. I think there are more New Yorkers going to this game than Cardinal fans. ASU is too much competition for the floundering red shirts.

When the gates finally opened I was handed a Safeway card which entitled me to free gifts if the Cardinals won. I later learned that I would have a free liter of Pepsi if I showed my stub at the nearest supermarket. I also received a ballot for the NFL pro bowl vote. Who was I going to vote for, Boomer Esiason or Dave Brown? There wasn't a player on the field worth his salary. But that's my New York cynicism. I spotted my seat but decided that I would drift around and walked to the fifty-yard line and up into the section.

I could hear the voice echoes of the few players warming up and the maybe 100 people scattered around the empty bowl. I saw a young girl wearing a yellow shirt indicating she was an usher or 'courtesy squad' as they called them here. I asked her if I could sit and watch the warm ups and she agreed. "Does the section usually fill up?"

"I don't know. This is my first game."

"Aha!" We were both virgins here. I sat and watched the kickers work out and then the squads amble onto the field and go through their drills. The crowd drifted in slowly. I was amazed to see nineteen kick line girls come out. I counted them. "My Arizona Cardinal cheerleaders," I was told. Wellington Mara, the Giants long time owner, would never permit any girls to shake their booties back home. New Yorkers have too much sophistication. We keep our tits and ass where they belong…in the boudoir or porno strip clubs! About fifteen minutes before game time about three-quarters of the section was filled. The end zone sections were crowded and the top deck empty. Maybe half the place would have spectators. The young usher asked me to please leave now. I offered her a few bucks to let me stay but she refused saying she could get into trouble. Ah, innocence! In Giants Stadium for ten bucks the usher would have gotten me a seat in the first row on the 50 yard line. I stood and walked down the aisle, shuffled over one section to the thirty-five and found an empty seat. Unfortunately it was on the aisle and there was a continuous flow of traffic up and down to the refreshment stalls and bathrooms. These people didn't want to watch football;

they wanted to drink beer, much like New York Ranger hockey fans. They wore an assortment of Cardinal red and white jerseys, shirts, hats and stood during every key play. I shouted "down in front" but it didn't work. I tried not to draw attention to myself since I was an interloper. An elderly couple sat in front of me. Later the man asked if anyone sat in the seat next to me. I didn't understand until he explained I was sitting in his seat but he'd rather stay in front of me because it was in the sun. I asked if he wanted to switch and he politely refused. He and his wife left after the first quarter and never returned. It puzzled me. I would die before I left a Giant game before the final whistle. So I ended up in a great seat, warm and sunny, watching my beloved Giants lose to a team their equal in ineptitude. There were fumbles, interceptions, missed tackles, and my Giants made Boomer Esiason look like a young all star. There was one drunken twenty year old with his girl friend who waved a Giants' banner constantly and yelled every time the Giants did something right. The courteous Cardinal fans looked at him as if he were some kind of creature from 'New Joisey." In the Meadowlands the guy would have been decked if he opened his mouth for the other side, girl friend or not! There was a continuous flow of commercial announcements over the public address system during the game and a contest to see if these two guys could throw a football through a 'Tru-value' hardware nut from five, ten and fifteen years away. One guy did it from five and ten but missed the big prize from fifteen. Two minutes before the end of the game there were announcements about the offensive player of the game (Boomer) and the defensive 'exterminator' (Seth Joyner). I got a kick out of Simeon Rice, rookie defensive end, dancing to the rock music during the time outs. His coach must be delighted at his professionalism.

The highlight for me was the half time show. In New Jersey they usually have some hack band like the Hawthorne Caballeros and everyone drinks beer and goes to the men's room. Here they had the University of

Arizona marching band and all the ASU fans booed and chanted "ASU" over and over. It was funny. Believe me, this place ain't the Meadowlands!

I guess the Giants enjoyed the sun as much as I did. They sure didn't come to play football. And Coach Dan Reeves looked dapper as ever in his tie and jacket, shades of his mentor, Tom Landry. I don't think he'll be visiting Phoenix again as the Giants coach.

The game ended with many of the fans having left before the end of the fourth quarter. I walked back to my car amid a lot of fathers and young sons and they made me feel good about remembering back to the time that I took my son, now a 28 year old doctor, to his first Giants' game. How hard we rooted and what a special day it was. I hoped these fathers and sons had that same kind of day.

For me this day had been new, unique…a nice afternoon, but not the way it used to be.

Eating out has been an adventure in dining. There is not a decent pizza place, Chinese restaurant or bakery in the valley. I sometimes need a pizza fix but to buy a slice I don't need a waitress to sit me at a table, bring me a knife and fork and have me wait twenty minutes to get a flat wedge of soggy, cardboard-like dough covered with Velveeta and Franco-American tomato sauce. Where is Ray's or Dominic's or even Goldberg's for a $1.50 slice of Sicilian served up in two minutes? When my neighbors sincerely extol the virtues of Pizza Hut I know I'm in trouble.

Won Ton soup costs $2.50 a bowl and you have to ask for noodles and tea in Phoenix's array of Oriental 'greasy spoons.' P.F. Chang's, allegedly Scottsdale's best, is like a Szechuan version of McDonald's in fancy surroundings. But you can't eat atmosphere. You get fried chicken nuggets smothered in celery and onions…and they don't serve brown rice!

I yearn for a good piece of chocolate layer cake, a legitimate Italian cannoli or a real cheese Danish. The bakery goods offered in the supermarkets are sad imitations of cakes sold in sterile, clear plastic containers, saturated with tons of sugar and flour tasting like airline food and costing outrageous prices. To eat one of these is to induce a diabetic seizure. Where are the pastry chefs of the valley? Twinkies and ding-dongs are not going to do it for me.

I have come to enjoy barbecue and 'wraps,' an ethnic accommodation to the sandwich, at various establishments around town. The burritos are scrumptious. I resent the Mexican restaurant chains, but the excellence of the local mom and pop eateries is second to none. My heavens, I'm putting on weight!

As for the high priced restaurants, many are located in hotels, which says a lot. I've become arrogant about my new roots and patronizing to tourists. After my experiences here can you believe my presumptuousness? The prolific California style restaurants offer a hundred varieties of hamburgers and mesquite grilled chicken sandwiches as well as salads. And so we are forced to frequent them. The alternative for a 'cheap feed,' the mall food courts, are as American as everywhere else be it Minneapolis or Omaha no less. Mall rats abound everywhere!

Manhattan has ten restaurants per city block, some inexpensive others costly…all different for better or for worse. Phoenix and vicinity has ten restaurants per square mile, clones of one another for better or worse. It'll take some getting used to but encourages eating at home. I feel sorry for the wife but at my age, cooking is a no no. My two years in the army with weekly K.P. killed my culinary creativity forever!

We are enjoying Arizona now, taking weekly day trips to new areas of our adopted state. New Yorkers always claim the Empire State is the most beautiful of the fifty. Remember 'I love New York'? But Arizona takes second place to none.

I don't want to be a typical New Yorker who never in his entire life visits the Statue of Liberty or the Empire State Building. Last summer, on a hot sultry day, I did visit Ellis Island for the first time in my life and was thrilled to participate in the excitement of a boatload of foreign tourists as they visited these American benchmark institutions. Their enthusiasm was contagious and made my day. I realize how foolish I was to have waited so long to discover these gems right on my doorstep.

Here in Arizona I have visited the red rocks of Sedona. When I saw them they made me gasp with wonder. I drove to the Grand Canyon, despising the honky-tonk carnival like atmosphere outside the park, but stunned by the beauty and majesty of this wonder of the world. I could have stared at it forever. It is mesmerizing in its grandeur.

We've traveled to Tucson, Tubac, Tombstone, the scene of so many of my favorite oaters, toured a copper mine in Bisbee. We've gone to Prescott's Whiskey Row, seen the natural bridge north of Payson. We've bought artwork in Jerome and loved its heights and views. Nogales, with its shops,offers Americans cheap pharmaceuticals, furnishings and other 'pleasures!' There are still hundreds of other places to visit and we have the luxury of time now. We won't be slackers!

20

Being there

As I sit in my Casbah home, I am comfortable and familiar with every part of it. It is my house with little pieces of all who helped put it together. Thinking back over the past months makes me smile as I remember the mischief of Roy, Stan and Don (the boys) as they greeted Mikey White Pants. The taste of conflicts with Brad the wallpaper man and the carpet installers remain. Each piece of furniture brings thoughts of Alan and Laurie and Karl. I still owe Tim Reilly a six pack. Jesus and Raul finally landscaped the yard and it was worth the wait.

I've learned the best places to shop, the delights of the state. I am coming to trust people again. I hope I'm losing my eastern cynicism and anxiety to the warmth of Southwestern Americans. I'm learning to slow down, to enjoy the sky which is a daily wonder especially at twilight. I even know the best golf courses, although not for playing, but for lunch. I love burritos and may qualify for the Guinness Book of Records if I keep devouring them at a stomach filling pace.

We may eventually work part time and have registered to start a real estate salesperson's three-week course. What the hell! Everyone else in this area seems to have a license!

Comparing New York and Arizona has been the center of this narrative. There are positives and negatives about both. But the one realization I've come to is that New York is New York and Arizona is Arizona. Brilliant conclusion! But you can't fairly compare the two with the idea of extolling the virtues of one to the detriment of the other. Each is unique and special and I appreciate that I'm lucky to have both. I look forward to going back to New York City for the holidays. Likewise, I will be glad to return to the valley. It's my home now. I'm no longer a stranger in a strange land. I've finally gotten to Phoenix!

The end

About the Author

Michael Boloker has lived in the New York City area all his life. He taught high school English for over 30 years and is a free lance writer. He has a wonderful marriage of 38 years to Judith. His son Judd is a physician and artist.

9 780595 187812